THE BRACK R

Brack held up a copy of the pamphlet.

'The pamphlet you will each have found on your chairs is a brief summary of the state of research into the enrichment of uranium by laser. It is classified information under the laws of this country, for the publication of which I expect to be arrested in a few minutes' time.

'You, ladies and gentlemen, are all witnesses to this act of criminal treason – and I hope that many of you will support me in this deliberate challenge to a diabolically restrictive and dangerous law.'

He relaxed for a moment and smiled, as if a huge burden had been removed from him, then straightened his back and stepped down towards the Special Branch men and the policeman, who were approaching.

'Now,' he asked calmly, 'how would you like this bit to happen?'

THE BRACK REPORT

a novel by
Patrick Winter

Based on the scripts of the Thames Television series *The Brack Report* by Christopher Penfold

Arrow Books

Arrow Books Limited
17–21 Conway Street, London W1P 6JD

An imprint of the Hutchinson Publishing Group

London Melbourne Sydney Auckland
Johannesburg and agencies
throughout the world

First published 1982

Set in Times by
Photobooks (Bristol) Limited
St Philips, Bristol

Made and printed in Great Britain
by The Anchor Press Ltd
Tiptree, Essex

ISBN 0 09 927160 5

1

The high barbed-wire fence sliced through the meadows overlooking Weymouth Bay, enclosing twenty acres of good Dorset farm land. As yet the grassland and hedgerows inside it were almost untouched; birds sang in the misty freshness of an early spring morning; plants pushed out shoots, trees nurtured their buds, oblivious of the fact that they would soon be crushed, cut down before summer came. The small cluster of caravans just inside the only gate in the fence showed no indication of human activity, but on the outside of the wire, where a gritted access-track led down to a country road, people were up and about. The siege of the Central Electricity Board's Heathbridge nuclear power station site was beginning another day.

Bleary-eyed figures shuffled between the tents, ageing dormobiles and cars grouped against the security barrier. A kettle whistled on a gaz stove. A teenage girl hung up washing on a makeshift line. One of the besiegers had hung a transistor radio on the central pole of a ridge tent, a harsh incursion into the stillness, telling the waking world that it could expect cloudy weather with showers and a few bright intervals.

A door opened, and a young policeman emerged from one of the caravans inside the wire, yawning as he surveyed the opposing campsite. His sleepy indifference moved in the direction of interest when he caught sight of the girl putting out her washing. She had a neat little backside, and her tight jeans showed it off to advantage. The policeman grinned appreciatively to himself. Nice. A hair-do, he thought, and some decent clothes, and he'd squire that one down the disco any night of the week. If, that was, his night off hadn't been cancelled, which these days was all too bloody likely. The slogan on the tee-shirt the girl was pegging up read: 'NO NUKES IS GOOD NUKES'. Ha bloody ha. And where the Electricity Board had put a large sign warning that 'Trespassers Will Be Prosecuted', those comedians had changed 'Prosecuted' to 'Irradiated'. The policeman stretched and yawned again. They could do what they liked out there, but one move through the wire and he and his mates would have them, tight jeans or no tight jeans. He was about to go back inside the caravan for his morning cup of tea when he noticed that a group of protesters was gathering round the radio slung up by the tent. The volume had been turned up.

'Hey, listen to this!' someone shouted. 'Radio Four, Tony Simpson. Hot stuff!'

The voice of the breakfast news show's anchorman oozed carefully modulated, neutral concern. He had mentioned the Heathbridge siege, then moved on to a book called *The Brack Report*, whose author was supposed to have 'set the cat among the nuclear pigeons'.

There was quite a large crowd listening to the radio by now, but the policeman quickly lost interest. The news item, whatever it was about, seemed to be exciting the great unwashed out there. Just so long as it didn't excite them too much. . . .

Pat Brack finished squeezing an orange, tipped the juice into the jug, then let herself down slowly onto a kitchen chair to listen to the anchorman's introduction of her husband.

'Dr Brack is here with me in the studio, and so is Sir Donald Parker on behalf of the Atomic Energy Authority . . .'

Then came the familiar voice, deceptively mild but with a touch of arrogance: 'I attack nuclear power on four fronts: economy, safety, security, and what I have called "social appropriateness". Basically, what I say is that nuclear power is proving a most expensive way of generating electricity which we do not really need . . .'

Pat stared out through the kitchen window. The garden had not been cared for during the winter, and it was in danger of becoming heavily overgrown. They had bought the rambling house in Oxford when Paul had still been working for the Atomic Energy Authority before he left to begin his crusade against nuclear power. It seemed strange and sad that he should be entering this house again through the tiny speaker of a cheap transistor radio.

'There is only one human activity with which it can be compared in terms of safety, and that is nuclear war,' he was saying. 'Because of the ease with which bombs can be made from nuclear materials, the proliferation of fission reactors has the same effect as the proliferation of nuclear weapons. Lastly, nuclear power is socially inappropriate because it consumes gargantuan amounts of capital but provides long-term employment for only a small, élite corps of highly specialized technicians.'

Pat nodded wryly. Paul Brack had never been one to gild his lily, even when they had been students together more than twenty years ago. He had always been the brilliant, wayward academic star, she more the solid, hard-working type. The contradictions had sharpened in trying to bring up two children and keep a marriage going while Paul had moved restlessly from project to project, job to job, with the Atomic Energy Authority, then for private nuclear interests in America, back to the UK again, until finally the strain had pulled them apart when Paul joined Harold Harlan's energy consultancy and promptly went riding off in every direction at once.

Her daughter, Angela, appeared in the doorway and made a face. 'Not interested,' she said. Pat shrugged and carried on listening. Angela had gone to wake Oliver, her brother, and tell him Dad was on the radio, obviously without much success. Angela was eighteen and Oliver two years younger, but they were almost as different as their mother and father. Where Angela strove to understand her parents with a maturity beyond her years, Oliver retreated into himself. Maybe he had been more vulnerable at the time of the breakup: his father, his idol, had suddenly acquired feet of clay and at sixteen that was hard to forgive. Bitterness and rejection of his father's values had been added to adolescent rebellion.

'Dad sounds almost reasonable,' Pat heard Angela say softly.

Her daughter was smiling encouragement, but Pat needed none. She smiled back as best she could and concentrated hard on the radio, hoping for a clue, something that would allow the gift of understanding that had always evaded her with Paul. It had not been anything sexual that had caused the breakup; only since then had Pat indulged herself in a little affaire – as had Paul, she gathered – and the effect of that had been merely to provide pleasant confirmation that she was still an attractive woman, despite the few grey hairs. No, it was a 'simple' matter of two minds that for the moment had ceased to communicate, however hard they tried. And as was usually the case with such 'simple' things, it was sad, messy and complex in ways that no outsider, not even one's own children, could understand.

Paul Brack spoke quickly and fluently into the microphone, his lean face earnest, forehead creased in a frown of concentration.

'Cheap oil,' he continued, 'caused us to abandon a host of alternative energy technologies and encouraged us to develop scandalously wasteful habits in consumption. The first positive alternative, therefore, is to make what we've got go twice as far.'

Tony Simpson saw his opportunity and moved in with another question.

'But surely that will only delay facing the real problem?'

Brack shook his head. 'Time is what we need, and in this respect the UK has been endowed by the Gods. We are an island of coal surrounded by a sea of oil. Proper management of these resources could keep us self-sufficient in energy for hundreds of years – time enough to consider and develop a whole range of renewable resources which would make our self-sufficiency permanent. But instead our policy is to lay all our eggs in the nuclear basket –'

'But are we not expected to be net importers of oil again by the end of the decade?'

'At present rates of consumption, yes,' Brack admitted.

'Ah . . . but none of your renewable technologies is going to put fuel in our petrol tanks by then, is it?'

'Nor is nuclear power!' Brack retorted firmly. 'There is simply no way we can avoid paying for the short-sightedness of the immediate past. If twenty-five nuclear power stations were magically to start generating electricity tomorrow, they'd do nothing to solve the underlying problem. In fact, they'd deepen it, because the vast amounts of our diminishing capital they consume would further reduce our ability to invest in renewable alternatives. And no one has investigated the fact that it takes an enormous amount of energy to keep a nuclear power station in operation. They simply don't bother to cost that factor –'

'Isn't there an element of a nostalgic hankering to return to the pre-industrial age dream of rural bliss?' Simpson cut in.

Brack glanced at him in irritation, almost forgetting the microphone. 'Look, I'm a scientist,' he answered. 'I believe that science has greatly enhanced the quality of many people's lives and that it can continue to do so. But it has also increased the dangers. Science provides choices, and people choose. Sometimes they choose wrong. The government of this country chose nuclear fission because they wanted plutonium to make bombs. The fact that the reactors could also be used to raise steam and generate electricity was a side-effect that sweetened the image of the atom at a time when the horrors of Hiroshima were fresher in people's minds than they are now. Nuclear fission is a crude, inefficient, uneconomic, dirty, dangerous and socially destabilizing way of generating electricity. It's a stunted science,' he declared passionately. 'A blind alley which has been promoted for the worst possible reasons . . .'

To his left, he noticed the presenter nod to Sir Donald Parker. The Atomic Energy Authority's spokesman responded with a satisfied smile. Simpson shifted position slightly and spread the fingers of both hands meaningfully. Ten seconds left, and Brack felt as if he had hardly begun.

'There are alternatives,' he said hastily. 'Fusion, for instance, in which I have research experience, could be the ultimate solution to our need for energy here on earth. Its primary fuels, deuterium and lithium, are readily available in virtually unlimited quantities. It is safe and clean. And that's not to mention wind power, biomass, fluidized bed combustion, all technologies in which spectacular advances have been made during the last few years. A massive transfer of resources, a change of public will is all that is needed. . . .'

Parker's lips were beginning to purse in irritated disapproval. Simpson's professional cool threatened to crack, but he saw his chance and leapt in before things got out of hand.

'Thank you, Dr Brack,' he said, moving on to the other interviewee without the kind of pause that might have enabled Brack to slot in another few sentences. 'Now, Sir Donald Parker, have you any comments on Dr Brack's accusations against nuclear power?'

Parker smiled his easiest smile. His bespoke suit and tie, made a neat contrast to Brack's chain-store sports jacket and open-necked shirt. Tidiness was his trademark. He had got to the top of the AEA's bureaucracy because the nuclear establishment had seen the value of a patrician intellect combined with the popular touch. Now he was about to justify his salary and the knighthood that went with it. His pleasant, dark-brown voice would have done credit to a voice-over in a cake commercial; the persona he liked to put over was that of a scientist who was also a sincere, no-nonsense sort of chap, doing what he thought best for Britain and tolerating no airy-fairy schemes.

'Certainly,' he began. 'Firstly, Dr Brack's . . . very diverse . . . arguments obscure one important fact, the most important one, I would submit. Namely that nuclear fission is already supplying some 14 per cent of the electricity we use in the United Kingdom. It is a very considerable bird in the hand.'

'And what about Dr Brack's allegation that nuclear fission is, I quote, "crude, inefficient, uneconomic, dirty, dangerous, and social destabilizing"?'

Parker laughed. 'Well, of course I can't agree with any of those rather emotive epithets,' he said comfortably. 'We have, of course, an absolutely magnificent safety record in the nuclear industry. None of the visitors to our nuclear installations could possibly describe them as in any way crude.'

The AEA spokesman was moving smoothly into overdrive. Simpson, nodding and casting wary glances at Brack, let him continue.

'As far as cost is concerned,' Parker said with another sardonic chuckle, very much that of the reasonable man astonished at a lunatic's inability to grasp the obvious, 'our first generation of Magnox reactors have consistently achieved the lowest all-in generating costs of any of the Electricity Board's power stations. And the second generation of Advanced Gas-Cooled reactors – like the one proposed at Heathbridge – should prove even more favourable from the economic point of view. Now the Fast Breeder Reactors – the third phase of our carefully-planned nuclear development – will make use of the plutonium produced in our present thermal reactors, thus saving more money, and they will provide as much electricity as we are likely to need for centuries to come . . .'

*

Several miles across London from the BBC radio studios, in a luxury flat at the top of a block in the Barbican, another man was listening to the interview with careful, not to say passionate, interest. Harold Harlan, founder and owner of Harlan International, Energy Consultants, was in his mid-forties, trim and crackling with a ruthless energy that belied his balding pate and cynical, world-weary eyes. British-born but schooled in the cut-throat world of the big American oil corporations, Harlan had invested in Paul Brack when the scientist had finally become disillusioned with nuclear power. The former President of Ensign Oil had given him time, money, backed him on more than one pet project, and this book, *The Brack Report* was Harlan's payoff, when he reckoned to start getting a real return on his investment. *The Brack Report* had been given the big treatment, publicity fanfares and copies to anyone who was anyone, as the spearhead of Harlan International's assault on conventional energy policy. And at the moment Harlan was not at all happy at the way Brack's first public exposure was going. In fact, he was beside himself with rage.

'Dammit!' he cursed, thumping the table in frustration. 'Why did we let Paul do this? Parker's having him for breakfast!'

On the other side of the breakfast table from him, his personal assistant – and lover – smiled coolly and nodded agreement. Sophie Ferris was blonde, beautiful, twenty-six years old, and very, very ambitious. She fed off Harlan's experience and dynamism, like a young animal gaining strength from a parent, and the nice thing about the relationship was that neither she nor her boss wanted any permanent strings. It was fun, convenient, easy: Sophie was too independent, Harlan too often divorced, to push things any further.

Sophie reached out one slim hand to console Harlan as Parker piled carefully selected statistic on carefully selected statistic, half-truth on half-truth, with no answer from Brack. Harlan ignored her. The confrontation was a simple matter of a professional trouncing an amateur, but that didn't make it any more bearable. Soon Harlan was on his feet, bawling at the radio:

'Hit back, man, for God's sake!'

Sir Donald Parker was summing up with his accustomed skill. He made no concessions in the face of Brack's increasingly heated signals to Simpson, who in any case was peering deliberately through the glass studio divide at his producer. Parker noted with relief that the producer was giving Simpson an emphatic wind-up cue. Another few seconds and he would be home and dry.

'That, then, is the crux of the argument,' he concluded. 'Positive achievement against supposition, the practically feasible against the theoretical. I'm sure Dr Brack's book is very admirable in many respects as a piece of futurology. If he, with his wealth of as yet unrealized alternatives, can produce a good reason why we should look the present gift-horse of nuclear technology in the mouth, then we might begin to have a sane discussion.'

Brack leaned forward, grimly determined, and took a deep breath, but the presenter was too experienced and too quick for him.

'Sir Donald Parker, Dr Brack, thank you,' Simpson said breezily. 'And now to the tranquil village of Chinnock in Leicestershire, where a new kind of potato has just made horticultural history . . .'

The smile that spread across Sir Donald's distinguished face exuded quiet triumph. Paul Brack's frustration was pleasantly apparent. Parker had earned his salary this morning. Then Brack shook his head wryly and, surprisingly enough, opened up with a broad, mischievous grin that almost matched his opponent's.

Simpson, his lead-in to the taped material from Leicestershire successfully accomplished, lifted off his headphones for a moment, drank some of his lukewarm coffee, and smiled appreciatively at the two interviewees.

'Terrific stuff,' he enthused. 'Should have the masses

sitting up in their Ford Cortinas and taking notice. Thanks again. The lovely lady over there is the producer's assistant, and she'll show you where to get some coffee if you feel the need.'

Then the headphones went back on and he was away, making sure the potato story was going okay and taking instructions from his producer. Parker and Brack were now surplus to requirements. For Christ's sake, this was peak-time radio, and most people were just waiting for news of the snarl-ups on the Kingston by-pass. The important thing was to keep moving, moving.

Harlan had his jacket on, ready to face the day. The breakfast mess had been cleared away. He led Paul Brack through into the living-room of the flat in sour silence, then turned on his heel.

'Well?' he said at last. 'Do I need to spell it out? Parker chewed you up and spat you out in little pieces within earshot of about five million people.'

'Thanks. But the interviewer –'

'He's a professional, Paul,' Harlan interrupted. 'Listen, the nuclear issue's been around for a while in one form or another. He's had good value from Parker in the past and he knows he'll get good value again if he treats him nicely. It's the way the system works . . . and you, Paul, are just a one-day wonder as far as Simpson's concerned.'

Brack frowned. 'Well, without any help from him I thought I scored quite a lot of points.'

'Quite right. The trouble is, they don't count if the other fellow wins by a knockout,' Harlan said acidly. 'I primed you, I warned you, but you still tried to spew a thousand pages in three minutes. He did the right thing and kept it tight and simple – at about groin level. How many ideas do you think people can swallow along with their cornflakes?' He sank back into a padded armchair and motioned for Brack to do the same. His eyes were hard. 'Okay,' he said with deceptive softness. 'You've had your big moment of glory. You know we have to find a political "in" somehow, and that's a delicate business. Take it easy and let me process the product.'

Harlan's final word touched a sore spot in Brack, as it was meant to. 'It's not a product!' he shot back, incensed.

'Ideas still have to be marketed if they're going to have any effect. It's about time you learnt that's not a dirty word.'

Brack snorted, unimpressed. 'Opinions are not pre-packaged commodities that you can sell to people,' he said stubbornly.

'Want to bet?'

Harlan was the first to break the angry silence that followed. 'We've tried, you and I – and the others – to awaken the public, to present them with feasible alternatives,' he said, adopting a more reasonable tone. 'We've worked our butts off this last couple of years, presenting facts until we're blue in the face, talking to people who count. But the other side have still got what we haven't: they can point to the status quo and say, we're part of it, and the status quo works. That's just what Parker did – all he had to do. Christ, Paul, he doesn't believe in all that crap. And do you think that most of the people out there know fission from fusion, a Darrieux aerogenerator from a hole in the wall . . .?'

Harlan knew Brack was itching to say his piece, but he put up one hand for silence. 'Bear with me, Paul, because what I'm saying you need to hear,' he said. 'You're a specialist, but don't tell me that the great British public really cares. Sure, when they bother to think about it they get the occasional shiver. Three Mile Island. New rumours about leaks at Windscale. But the rest of the time they've got their cars, their TVs, their hi-fis and the rest of their energy-hungry home comforts, Paul, and they feel they can't live without them. And who are you and me to tell them nay?' He waved a hand around his gadget-filled flat. 'I like that stuff just as much as everyone does. And Parker sure as hell isn't going to tell them they have to be good conservationists. Oh no: he's going to sit there and state fairly, objectively, conclusively, that the nuclear way is the only viable way. And people are going to believe him – though you and I know it's rubbish – because they've been hearing it for thirty years and because he's very good at making us look like a bunch of woolly-minded cranks. We need to counter that, by being as slick, pushy, and, if you like, unprincipled as the enemy. I rest my case.'

Brack sat thoughtfully for a few moments, then shook his head. 'Harold, I still refuse to accept what you say. Speaking for myself, I must be able to believe in the possibility of offering people facts, engaging them in debate and persuading them, by reasoned argument, to change their minds.'

'We all have our problems,' Harlan growled. 'As far as you're concerned, mine is that I'm a capitalist, ex-oil company chief who's out to exploit alternative energy sources for profit, because he sees the way the wind's blowing. You're quite right, of course, in your basic assumption, but wrong in supposing that because of that I'm disqualified from acting as an effective instrument for socially beneficial change.' He grinned, pleased with his turn of phrase. 'I get things done, Paul,' Harlan said bluntly. 'That's my trump card. People like you need people like me.'

'And the *Report*' Brack asked. 'I'm supposed to leave you to sell it like soap?'

'You know what I think of the book,' Harlan answered soothingly. 'It's superb. Okay,' he added, and the hard look came back into his eyes. 'But now you have to leave it as a weapon in my hands.'

The look on Brack's face was still sceptical, even anxious. Harlan stood up, avoiding the force of the scientist's distrust by sauntering over to the window with a casualness that fooled neither of them.

'Paul,' he said. 'You remember where we first met and talked about your working for Harlan International?'

Brack nodded. He could see what was coming.

'At Max Challen's place – which should have given you

some idea of what kind of animal you were dealing with,' he answered, heading off Harlan's all-too-clear line of advance.

Harlan shrugged in acknowledgement, but he was thick-skinned enough to press on.

'You know I'm very fond of Maxwell. There's an awful lot to admire in the man,' he said. 'That's why I was there at his mill-house – apart from head-hunting for the likes of you.' He paused. 'What I want to say, though, is that I really don't want Paul Brack to go the same way Challen has. It's a luxury neither you nor I can afford. Okay, the old boy stored up a lot of credit for himself: the Manhattan Project, work at Calder Hall, a dazzlingly original research record. Then, after twenty years as a top dog, he brings the whole thing down around himself. He leaves the AEA and rounds on everything he ever stood for, becomes what they used to call a "peacenik", crying for the end of the whole dirty game, an era of East–West co-operation –'

'If you're trying to tell me he's wrong . . .' Brack interrupted with a new sharpness in his voice.

When, after the near-disaster at the Wintersham nuclear reactor and the official refusal to admit its mistakes, Brack had finally decided that he could no longer accept the Atomic Energy Authority's rules, he had looked up Maxwell Challen. His conversations with the scientific elder statesman of the anti-nuclear movement had helped him to make up his mind to leave. And the experience itself had been precious to him, like a brief meeting with a rational, lucid mind in a room full of madmen.

Harlan looked at him for a long moment, smiling, then said: 'How could I say he's wrong? Maxwell is absolutely right. Just like the good people who keep telling us to give up smoking, or stop taking drugs, or stealing, or committing violence against our fellow human beings. It's not the message, Paul, it's the way you put that message over that counts – particularly when you're in the business of stating the obvious.'

'Challen's still very much alive and kicking. And perhaps

more people are listening these days. Like me – and even you . . .' Brack retorted defiantly.

Harlan shook his head. 'Challen stopped influencing the people who count when he went right over the top in the early sixties,' he said. 'He's still around and in a position to make a noise because his industrialist father left him with a private fortune. He can afford to indulge himself, Paul – and we can't. We're two lads from humble backgrounds who've made it to a position where we could just conceivably make a difference. Whatever our different views about what precisely to do with our power, we should remember that. It only takes one more false step to put us out of business.'

It was Brack's turn to be cynical. 'Put *you* out of business, you mean, Harold,' he said. 'And I fail to see what this working-class-boy-made-good nonsense has to do with thc argument. It's a bigger thing than that; it's about truth, and honesty, and about the future of the entire human race – Harlan International included . . .'

'And that's exactly why we have to take it out of the hands of well-meaning, clumsy amateurs!' Harlan shot back at him in a sudden blaze of anger. Then he turned back to the window, and spoke patiently. 'It's a frightened world we live in today, Paul,' he continued. 'It doesn't matter whether you're in London or Los Angeles, Djakarta or – for Christ's sake – Dnepropetrovsk. Energy is the key to political power; it's the cement that holds our cosy way of life together, and that whole way of life is under threat.'

'As Maxwell once said to me, at this rate life may no longer be worth living, any way at all,' Brack muttered.

Harlan nodded expansively, though whether he was signalling agreement with Brack or simply trying to placate him, it was hard to tell.

'Just never forget that when he went over to the fringe, his best work was behind him. I like to think yours is still to come,' he said. He smiled genially. 'Your wonderful, ridiculous idealism is part of the reason I like you, Paul. There may be a few others operating on the same wavelength, and they're the ones who'll understand. But the opinions we need to change at the moment are those of the people who run things, who make the decisions. And, as we've found out to our cost, the last quality you can expect in a politician is an open mind – they want votes, and easy options. So, please: you've given us a weapon with this book of yours. Now leave the corridors of power to me and take it easy . . .'

'Does that mean I'm still allowed to do the TV interview this afternoon?' Brack said.

Harlan ignored the patent sarcasm of the question.

'Of course. Essential,' he said, stepping back into the middle of the room. 'And naturally I'll be there to help, right behind you every inch of the way.'

2

The view from the ministerial suite on the top floor of the Millbank Tower was stunning, in a distinctly inhuman sort of way. The office blocks clustering in the City looked stunted and oddly vulnerable from here, Norman Phillips thought, reminiscent of the cardboard buildings that used to go with his boyhood train sets. Even the green hills of Hertfordshire, visible twenty miles away to the north, seemed to lack substance, like papier-mâché scenery. As he listened, nodding, to the voice of the Secretary of State for Energy detailing why the Atomic Energy Authority need fear nothing from *The Brack Report*, Norman Phillips wondered idly whether some enterprising modern psychologist had ever done a study on the effect of skyscraper living on business tycoons and powerful politicians. It was not hard to believe that a man who spent his working existence in this eyrie-like environment might become infected with a touch of unreality, even megalomania. An interesting idea. *Folie de Grandeur: The Architectural Factor* would make a plausible title. . . .

Phillips turned away from the panoramic window to face the Minister.

'A burnt-out case, of course,' Basil Braintree blustered on. 'He's turned himself into a scientific outcast.'

The AEA chief shook his head. 'I don't think I can really agree with such a simplified view of Brack's capabilities,' he said. 'The man did some very good, even superb work for us, and we were sorry to lose him. Certainly he's a thorny character, but then most original minds are. As you may know, I still had hopes he would lead our fusion research at Culham until . . . ah . . . that unfortunate business a while ago. . . .'

Braintree looked at him sharply. 'You mean the Tchenkov affair?'

'I would guess that has a good deal to do with Brack's present attitudes towards the AEA,' Phillips confirmed, settling his tall frame into an easy chair opposite the Minister. 'Tchenkov's ideas were far in advance of anything we had, and he wanted to work here – preferably with Brack. Trading him off to the Americans was a purely political move. Brack took it hard because he knew and admired Tchenkov, but he wasn't the only one to feel uneasy. There were plenty of others at the AEA and elsewhere who were none too pleased about it either.'

Braintree rode the rebuke. The defecting Russian fusion expert had been debriefed by Brack and a female colleague from the AEA before being sent off to the States. After all, the Yanks wanted Tchenkov and Britain was deep in hock to them for nuclear technology, so the deal had been quite normal and logical. When someone defected, they had to take their chances. Currently Tchenkov was on an enormous salary at Princeton, with almost unlimited research funds, which hardly counted as a fate worse than death. Certainly Phillips had disapproved of the whole thing, but he had done nothing about it at the time. Why the snide complaints now?

'As you know, we had very little choice in the matter, as is often the case in our dealings with the Americans,' Braintree answered smoothly. 'Unfortunate I grant you, but if one silly book is the only price we have to pay, then I think we can count ourselves pretty lucky, Norman.'

Phillips frowned. 'Have you actually read *The Brack Report*, Basil?' he asked.

'Skimmed, skimmed. Found it rather hard going. But I've been well briefed, of course.'

'By Sir Frank Sampson?'

'He had a summary put together, yes. . . .'

Phillips said nothing about that, though the knowledge that Braintree's Permanent Secretary had been his main source said a lot. Sampson, departmental head under the last three governments, was a real hardliner on the nuclear issue, perhaps even more so than the AEA itself. 'Well,' Phillips said. 'I have looked at it pretty thoroughly, and we don't come out of it very well, I'm afraid.'

The Minister was displeased. 'Good Lord, Norman. You sound as though you believe that Brack actually has a case!'

O holy simplicity, Phillips thought wearily. In the minds of men like Braintree one was either wholly right or wholly wrong, cops and robbers, heroes and villains. Even after years of liaising with the AEA's political masters Phillips had never quite got used to their way of thinking. He could manipulate it to the Authority's advantage at times, and had become adept at behaving as if he lived in their world, but in much the same way as one might speak a foreign language fluently enough to pass as a native without actually being absorbed by the alien culture. A scientific training marked one for life.

'Oh, he can make one all right,' he told the Minister with untypical bluntness. 'He's come up with some damning statistics, and his surveys of the alternatives are cogent, authoritative and based on the latest research – some of it his own.'

Braintree's answering smile held a hint of superiority, the confidence of an experienced political infighter with expert civil servants at his beck and call and more than enough nous to send any troublesome interloper packing.

'I heard Brack on the radio this morning on my way here,' he said with barely-concealed contempt. 'I don't think we need panic yet. Parker handled him pretty well.'

'He did,' Phillips conceded.

'Well, there you are,' the Minister said, leaning forward across his desk like a headmaster confiding in a prize pupil. 'In fact,' he added, 'I'm scheduled to answer a question in the House this afternoon from that chap Morgan Ellis, spokesman for the alternative energy crowd. I had been intending to give a standard answer, but I think perhaps I shall go for the jugular under the circumstances. It will be an excellent opportunity for me to reaffirm our absolute commitment to nuclear expansion.'

Phillips looked at him doubtfully. Of course it was good to know that one enjoyed the Minister's unflinching support, but on the other hand it was possible that Braintree's gung-ho approach would do more harm than good. *The Brack Report* was more than another wishy-washy compendium of romantic notions; Phillips kept closely enough in touch with the scientific community at large to know that Brack's book would be read and inwardly digested by some very clever and influential people, who might draw conclusions highly unfavourable to the nuclear cause. There, as far as he was concerned, was where the real danger lay, and to that extent Brack's capacity to impress breakfast-time radio audiences was only part of the story.

'I would be a little careful, nevertheless, Basil,' he counselled, choosing his words with caution.

'Of what?' the Minister said. 'Or rather, of whom? Really, Norman, you're turning this Brack chap into some kind of bête noire. Come on – there will always be scientists who go off the deep end. They're an unreliable lot. . . .'

'Brack is not run-of-the-mill. He's done some brilliant work, he's still at the height of his powers. Whatever his failings as a PR man, I feel I should make it clear that he makes a bad enemy. He's as fierce as a bulldog when roused – and just as tenacious,' Phillips told him stubbornly.

'Know him well, do you?'

'Well enough.'

There was an edgy stand-off. Phillips could have gone further. He knew a bit about dissident scientists. Twenty years before, Maxwell Challen had left the Atomic Energy Authority in a blaze of publicity. And Max's wife, Evelyn, had left her husband for Norman Phillips. He had been married to Evelyn for two decades, and had acted as stepfather to hers and Max's daughter, Sarah – now herself a research scientist with the AEA. Sarah in turn had worked with Paul Brack on the Tchenkov debriefing, and the two of them had been lovers since Brack and his wife had separated. A tangled web, a mess. Yes, Norman Phillips knew something about Brack – more than he was prepared to tell the Minister.

'Remember also that anyone who's against, or even wavering on the nuclear power issue will have been thoroughly primed by Harold Harlan,' Phillips said to break the stalemate.

Braintree snorted with cynical satisfaction. Now Harold Harlan was a man he could understand, a wheeler-dealer.

'Absolutely,' he said. 'Friend Harlan has a big investment at stake.'

The Minister glanced surreptitiously at the clock on the wall, then stood and put a hand on Phillips's shoulder. It was a gesture both of encouragement and dismissal.

'Thank you, Norman. But don't worry. Harlan's too keen on gaining the governmental ear to push things too far.' He chortled. 'You just leave him to me, eh?'

'All right,' Phillips sighed, rising from his chair. 'But I urge you not to underestimate Brack, either. He's a firebrand. And because of his long connections with both fission and fusion research, he possesses a good deal of information which does us no credit at all.'

'Ah, but all classified, I presume?' Braintree answered silkily, his hand already on the door-knob.

Phillips nodded grimly.

'And that could just prove a major embarrassment in itself,' he warned.

The smile, however, did not leave the Minister's face. And the door was already open.

Sophie Ferris was entertaining Morgan Ellis, MP, to pre-lunch drinks when Harlan made his entrance into the living room of the flat. As usual, she had the man twisted round her delicate little finger, he noted with approval. Her blouse was open the regulation two buttons, and her bright eyes sparkled with an extra, professionally flirtatious gleam. It was lucky that he was not a jealous man; after a couple of divorces and a lot of other women, he preferred his sex friendly and easy with no strings.

Sophie and Ellis were guffawing over an insider's joke. Harlan grinned and shook the young MP's hand. Sophie quickly disengaged and went to fix his habitual pre-lunch Scotch, like any good PA – or mistress.

'How are you Harold?' Ellis asked. 'Nice piece on the radio this morning.'

Harlan grimaced. 'Don't bullshit, Morgan,' he growled. 'Paul was buried.'

'Oh, I wouldn't say that . . .' Morgan Ellis was in his mid-thirties, one of the brightest among the Opposition's most recent parliamentary intake, with a seat in the industrial north that had to be as safe as the Rock of Gibraltar. He had the kind of qualifications that promised a successful career: he was enough of a working-class boy made good to have solid appeal to his constituents, fashionable enough in his thinking to gain influence in the middle-class pressure groups. In short, he was precisely the kind of ambitious potential star who could do Harlan-Brack a lot of good – so long as the second half of the partnership didn't do too much damage before Harlan had prepared the political ground . . .

Sophie handed Harlan his drink and announced that lunch was ready.

'Thanks, darling,' Harlan said. 'We'll be through in a minute.'

Ellis watched her with unconcealed appreciation as she went back through to the dining room.

'I'm impressed,' the MP murmured, with considerably more sincerity than he had been able to muster in the brief discussion of the radio interview.

'I can practically smell that,' Harlan answered with a fond and ever-so-slightly proprietorial grin.

'Ambitious, too. Really fancies herself in the corridors of power.'

Harlan chuckled. 'She's already in the corridors, Morgan,' he said. 'What she wants is centre-stage.' He paused to take a sip of his whisky, and his manner changed abruptly. 'Well?'

'Yes . . . well . . .' Ellis said, disconcerted by the sudden end to the preliminary chat, though he knew Harlan well enough to know that it was one of the man's favourite gambits. 'I've sounded out a cross-section of opinion and the response has been very favourable.'

'How favourable?'

'The feeling is that Paul's Report provides sufficient grounds to demand an emergency debate.'

Harlan nodded, as if it were no more than his due. 'So will you go for that this afternoon?'

'I intend to try.'

'Okay,' Harlan said crisply. 'Now, how could you also handle a conservatively argued case that between 1970 and 1990 the nuclear programme will have accumulated losses of up to eight and a half thousand million pounds without adding one kilowatt to the national grid?'

Ellis whistled and looked at him in unfeigned amazement. 'Who's responsible for that?'

'We are. In conjunction with the Oxford Economic Forecasting Group – Professor Ayling's merry men.' Harlan smiled at the MP. 'We've only had a preview as yet, but it's already been enough to get the Commons Select Committee reconvened.'

He rocked back on his heels and busied himself with his drink, letting the news sink in and giving the MP time to hear the wheels in motion.

Ellis was obviously impressed – and maybe a little put out that he had to hear the news about the Select Committee from Harlan. 'And how much must all this be costing you, Harold?' he asked softly.

'A lot. But only a fraction of what I intend to get my hands on when nuclear capital expenditure is eventually reallocated,' Harlan said. He flashed the MP a broad, piratical smile that exuded complete self-assurance. 'There aren't many occasions when commercial advantage is consistent with the public good – as your lot never tire of telling us,' he jibed good-humouredly. 'But now I've found one, I'll stop at nothing to make it work.'

Harlan downed his whisky in one gulp and took the bemused politician by the arm to steer him through into the dining room.

'This,' he said. 'Is just the kick-off. Come on, let's eat. . . .'

The phone in the kitchen of the house in Oxford had been ringing for some time before the sound was overlaid by the scraping of a key in the door and Pat Brack's anxious voice.

'Quick, Ollie, answer it, please. . . .'

Her son burst in and loped for the phone, dropping his squash bag as he ran. Pat followed wearily, shut the door and set down her briefcase and shopping bag before bracing herself to go through and take the call. She met Oliver at the kitchen door, and he made an empty-handed gesture.

'Sorry,' he said. 'Too late.' His look became searching when he saw disappointment etched in her face. 'Were you expecting it to be Dad?'

'Yes . . . yes . . .' Pat answered slowly, 'I suppose I was.' She had a bleak sense of her life being an open book to her children.

'Why don't you ring him?' Oliver said.

Pat smiled painfully. A book open to be read, perhaps, but not completely understood. How did you explain? 'Oh, he's got interviews today,' she murmured vaguely. 'A press conference. The TV programme . . .'

'He's always got something,' Oliver said, mooching over to the kitchen table. He picked up the copy of his father's book that had arrived that morning and gave it a cursory flick-through. 'What's it like?'

The question was abrupt, almost a challenge, and it was

a challenge Pat Brack didn't feel she could handle at the moment.

'Oh, you know, brilliant as usual,' she said with an attempt at a bright smile. 'You should read it. Actually, it's not what you might call usual at all.'

Oliver tossed the book back on the table. His face had that awful blank look it seemed to wear so often these days. He said nothing. Pat gave up and began to pack his sweat-stained squash kit into the washing machine. Only then did her son speak.

'Will he come home now that his Report's been published?'

She did not turn round. 'I can't say . . .' she said, trying to sound matter-of-fact. 'We did discuss the possibility.'

'And?' The boy's tone was relentless, like an interrogator.

'I don't know, Ollie. . . .'

Pat turned to face him, mechanically pressing the start button of the machine, and rested for a moment against the work surface. Oliver was standing with his arms folded, half accusing, half pleading.

'Your attitude's changed a lot, though, hasn't it?' he said.

'In what way?'

Oliver shook his head in exasperation. 'You're supporting him again, being defensive. What changed your mind?'

Pat, however, was already filling the kettle from the sink. 'Do you want a cup of tea?' she asked.

'Yes, please – and an answer to my question.'

When she plugged in the kettle and began to unpack the shopping, he stepped over quickly and moved the bag out of her reach with something close to violence.

'Answer me, Mum,' he said urgently. 'I want to know.'

And so Pat had to face him. Oliver was right, she knew, to demand explanations, but it was hard when she didn't know all the answers, or even the connections, herself.

'I think, Ollie, that I've been living for years with an idea . . .' she began haltingly, taking up an awkward perch on one of the breakfast stools. 'The idea . . . subconscious, I hope, or I'd have no excuse for not facing it sooner . . . that your father was . . .' she groped for the word, hoping she could find something that didn't make it sound too cheap, even to herself 'was a potential star in the scientific Pantheon. Well, I think it was the Tchenkov business that finally shook my faith in the religion of science and see what made your father really tick. It – well, it made me realize how little importance was attached to purely intellectual endeavour in the real world, and how much more important were ordinary human failings like ruthless ambition, commercial greed and the pursuit of power . . .'

'So you think that's what Dad's been involved in?'

'I'm beginning to accept that . . . well, political change has to come first. So that science can be better directed, better applied.'

Oliver tossed his shock of hair sceptically. 'And how do you suggest we bring about that political change?'

'In the end, Ollie, you do it yourself,' she said. 'With anyone else who's willing to help.'

Her phrases felt lame and tired before she had finished speaking, but it was as close to what she thought to be the truth – the only answer – as she could get. Neither her intellectual nor her emotional defences could protect her against the bruising power of Oliver's response.

'If you ask me,' he snapped. 'You've just swapped one facile faith for another. What I want to know,' he said with a raw anger that was almost physically overwhelming, 'is how d'you make out with no faith at all?'

Pat could find nothing to say. The cut went too deep. She had gone to university, married, made a career. There had been problems, pains, but somehow there had always been some hope of finding answers that would make things better. Now the child she had borne and brought up was saying that hope was an illusion – and meaning it, out of his own experience meaning it.

She was coming close to tears when she heard Oliver's voice, softer now, say: 'Anyway, what's that got to do with Dad coming home?'

*

Harlan and Sophie Ferris sat close together in the public gallery of the House of Commons. The chamber was well-filled, and there was a good turnout in the gallery as well; Harlan had primed both MPs and the media with his customary efficiency.

'You can see Braintree's teensy bald patch from here,' Sophie whispered with a malicious giggle.

Harlan grinned. 'There's one or two other blank areas showing, too,' he hissed back.

At the dispatch box the Energy Secretary was reaching the climax of his answer to the question Ellis had tabled regarding nuclear policy, and he was laying it on with a trowel.

'This administration will not flinch from its duty to the British people,' he intoned. '*We* are not afraid to take unpopular decisions now, in the knowledge that we shall reap no reward for a decade.' He paused dramatically and stared in the direction of the Opposition benches, in a way that implied that they would sell their sons and daughters into slavery for a handful of Siberian gold. 'Because,' he continued, 'it will take that long before the current generation of nuclear power stations will be ready to supply energy. But the fact that we shall, by then, be desperate for it is a fact for which we have to blame the irresponsible negligence of the previous government.'

The House echoed to loud Opposition boos and shouts of 'cheap!', mingled with a counter-barrage of dutiful cheers from the government benches. Despite shouts of 'Order!' from the Speaker, it was some time before the wave of noise had subsided sufficiently for Braintree to resume his answer.

'It is in this context, therefore, that I answer my honourable friend,' he continued. 'No, there will be no reconsideration of a nuclear policy to which this government is resolutely and even irrevocably committed. We have absolute confidence in both the economics and the safety of nuclear power, and we shall not be afraid to take any action that might be necessary to maintain the security of this, the most vital aspect of our nation's future!'

Braintree resumed his seat on the front bench with a triumphant smirk, to a tide of catcalls and, at the end, surprisingly sparse cheers from his own party ranks. Morgan Ellis was on his feet immediately, waving his order paper to gain the Speaker's attention.

'Supplementary from the Honourable Member for Southcote East,' the Speaker said.

The young MP had to raise his voice above the angry murmurings, but he was a powerful speaker and Harlan could hear him clearly from the gallery.

'In his answer, the Right Honourable Minister gives no indication of having read the remarkable book, *The Brack Report*, which has just been published. Is he even aware,' Ellis glowered, 'that the book contains compellingly authoritative refutations of every single premise on which this government's nuclear policy is based? And further that the author presents a detailed plan for an alternative way that is not only economically credible but also socially and environmentally attractive? And in the light of such arguments would not the Right Honourable Minister deem it wise to think again about his arrogant and dogmatic refusal to reconsider?'

The question brought a renewed chorus of approval, again with very few opposing voices. Harlan and Sophie Ferris exchanged satisfied smiles in the gallery.

Braintree, who had been ostentatiously adjusting the carnation in his lapel throughout Ellis's question, returned to the dispatch box with a long-suffering look.

'It may be,' he said airily, 'that previous administrations have made a practice of allowing themselves to be influenced by any twopenny-halfpenny publication blowing about in the fickle winds of liberal fashion, but . . .' The cries of 'Shame! Shame!' and 'Answer! Answer!' forced him to break off, but the Minister stood his ground, staring straight ahead while the Speaker restored order. Then he drew a deep breath. 'If I may offer my answer to the

Honourable Member in the briefest possible way,' Braintree concluded with insulting precision. 'It is: "No!"'

During the ensuing uproar, as members from both parties leapt to their feet waving order papers, Harlan patted Sophie's hand.

'Ellis is doing fine – or as well as you can do in this bear garden,' he said. 'But that toffee-nosed bastard Braintree is our best ally.' His chuckle was deep and rich with enjoyment. 'Hey, I believe we're on our way, kid. . . .'

Paul Brack's office was spacious. Harlan had provided him with a generous-sized desk; ranks of filing cabinets lined the walls; the room was expensively carpeted. None of these things prevented his working quarters from being as chaotic as any postgraduate student's cubby-hole. Sheafs of notes were stacked perilously on all available surfaces, files were piled on the carpet, charts and diagrams overflowed from the pin-board and onto the walls. The computer keyboard on his desk was almost submerged under a sea of papers.

Returning to Waldegrave House had probably been a mistake, Brack decided. His spirits had started to sag during the ninety-minute train journey from London, and by the time he had collected his bike from the station and pedalled to Harlan International's headquarters, the feeling of deflation had become like a dead weight on his mind. He stared morosely out into the darkness, then steeled himself to continue attempting to bring some sort of order to his desk. It was no good. Sure, he had brought his precious *Report* into the world and it was time for a spring clean. And how did it feel? Triumphant? Was there cause for relief, celebration? There had been the novelty of the radio interview, the press conference and the TV interview, and now – a hollowness, almost a sense of being tainted. *The Brack Report* was his no longer, he had given birth to his brainchild. Now he had to sit by and watch it launched out into the dangerous territory outside his mind, to be abused, used, attacked, misunderstood, while all the time he knew it wasn't enough, didn't really say what he had wanted to say. Christ, it was just grist to the mill, another item in the tool-bag that Harlan was filling, ready to prise open the government's energy coffers. . . .

A copy lay on the desk. Brack gazed at it with distaste. Suddenly he wanted it out of his sight, a parent embarrassed by an unattractive offspring.

He heard a knock on the door. In marched Ellie, the cleaning lady, to empty his waste-paper bin. It was the only thing in his office she was allowed to touch, a fact which caused her great professional pain. Brack smiled absently as she tipped the overflowing bin into her black plastic sack, but Ellie wasn't going to let him get away unchided tonight.

'Think we may be able to have a bit of a clean-up now, Dr Brack?' she said, amiably but with a hint of reproach.

Brack grinned, grateful for human simplicity. 'Tomorrow you're welcome to come in and whirl around like a white tornado,' he said.

Ellie stopped shaking her sack.

'Be taking a holiday now, will you?' she asked sympathetically.

'You're not the first to suggest it.'

Ellie sighed and shook her head in kindly despair. She knew Brack well enough to realize that any advice in that direction had been rejected. 'Well,' she told him stoutly. 'I'll be watching the telly tonight, Dr Brack. It is right that you'll be on, isn't it?'

Brack nodded wryly. 'Provided Mr Greedy of Grantham hasn't just broken the world record for non-stop porridge-eating.'

'Well, I'll be watching, anyway,' Ellie said. She smiled at him rather sadly, as if to say: you're clever, and now you're famous, but what have you really got that's precious? Then she shuffled towards the door, still shaking her head. 'Good night,' she called.

'Good night . . .'

Alone again, Brack sat for a moment staring listlessly at

the closed door. Suddenly he remembered the newly emptied waste bin, grinned to himself, stood with the copy of his book in his hand, judged his distance and tossed *The Brack Report* in a graceful parabola, straight into the vacant bin. In the same burst of energy, he picked up his briefcase and snapped the clasp shut. Time to go. The report, even maybe this office and his work with Harlan were done, more of the past than the future. In an odd sort of way, it was much older relationships that were in need of renewal . . .

The telephone was tempting. Pat had been out when he had rung earlier. With *The Brack Report* finally seeing the light of – he smiled bitterly – the waste bin, they might have something to say to each other. His wife had been right about Harlan when she had described him as – what was it? – 'a predatory animal, quick and without conscience'. Mind you, she had also summed Brack himself up as a 'contentious old dog whom people let out to bark', which tended to even up the insult score. There was truth in both comments, as usual with Pat. But as for the 'old dog' bit, Brack had already decided he had to do something about that one.

He stared at the telephone for a few seconds, then decided against ringing Oxford. Too many things could go wrong, and he was tired and hungry. Better to go back to his flat in Waldegrave and get some rest. The bike ride would clear his head, and the Kentucky Fried Chicken place in the High Street would still be open for his usual. . .

3

The ITN newsreader moved smoothly into the scheduled item: 'And tonight we bring the first of a series of special reports on the background to the Heathbridge Inquiry. Nick Rowe takes a look at the anti-nuclear movement. . . .'

The viewers went over to the Dorset power station site siege and shots of the motley array of protesting groups, but up in the director's gallery overlooking the studio they were busy with new material that had just come in. Silent film of the Brack interview recorded earlier in the day was being given a run through.

'We'll use that film of Brack,' the director said crisply. 'Then we'll take an intro from Sandy, and then over to Jonathan at Westminster.'

A glance at another of the battery of monitors told him that Jonathan Hawker, ITN's parliamentary correspondent, was ready in the Westminster studio. The director pressed a key to speak to him.

'How is it, Jonathan?'

The reporter grinned. 'Sensational's the word, I think.'

'Okay. Stand by. We'll be coming back to you in about one minute thirty.'

He checked on the situation with the film report. Fine: Rowe was talking in front of the Dungeness 'B' nuclear power station, still uncompleted after more than a decade of trial and error – mostly error. The director was able to speak directly to the news reader.

'Okay, Sandy?' he said. 'There've been developments on the nuclear issue at Westminster which dovetail in nicely.

We're using Jonathan. Straight in after the Brack film.'

The newsreader peered upward towards the gallery. 'Fine. Just give me the words.'

'Oh . . . something like . . . "While we've been on the air there's been a sensational development on the nuclear issue in the House of Commons." Then introduce Jonathan.'

The newsreader nodded, took a sip of water and straightened his tie. The special report material had only a few seconds still to run. His features were already composing themselves into the obligatory bland mask by the time the report came to an end and the monitors flashed up the intense face of Paul Brack.

Brack's flat was not much tidier than his office, but he did manage to preserve some of the domestic decencies. The chicken, along with its small cardboard carton of what the man at the place in the High Street always insisted on calling 'fries', had been transferred to a plate. A beer had been fetched from the fridge and poured into a glass.

Perhaps Brack had registered the raucous sound of a motor-cycle coming up the drive towards the flat. If so, the signal had stayed firmly in his subconscious. He was surprised to hear the door-bell ring and even more surprised when he rose, half-eaten drumstick in one hand, slid back the latch and saw his daughter burst into the room.

Resplendent in leathers with a helmet tucked under her arm, Angela kissed him in passing, then headed for the television set in the corner, with a cheerful cry of: 'Hello, Dad. Nipped across on the bike. Am I too late?'

'Too late for what?' he murmured with a bemused smile. It was only about half an hour's drive from Oxford to Waldegrave. Since his daughter had notched up another milestone in her liberation by acquiring a near-vintage bike, she had made the trip quite often, usually on errands of peace and conciliation. They made a joke of it: she was known as 'the Brack family's Henry Kissinger'.

But Brack had no time to ask her business at this time in

the evening. 'Oh, God, that's typical!' she bawled fondly as the TV flickered into life and a shot of her father talking to Nick Rowe appeared on the screen.

Brack closed the door and watched with her for a few minutes. Then, almost stealthily, he picked up his plate and returned to his dinner.

'The nuclear problem in this country grew out of the bomb,' he heard himself saying on the screen. 'There has never been a clear distinction between military and civil nuclear activity. The UKAEA is the administrative body for all things nuclear, and the cloak of official secrecy covers all. As a result there has never been an open public debate on the central issue. That is: whether or not we, as a people, desire to commit ourselves to a nuclear future. We need that debate.'

The face faded from the screen and was replaced by the newsreader back in the studio. Within seconds Brack found himself facing a sustained bout of hugs and kisses from his eighteen-year-old daughter.

'Terrific, Dad. Well done!' she squealed between kisses.

He tried to smile. It was good to see her. But that interview was already history.

'Glad you appreciate your old dad sometimes,' he forced himself to say. 'Have a drink. . . .'

The ITN director watched his transmission monitor, where the newsreader was completing his introduction to the parliamentary coverage.

'Here, live from Westminster, is our parliamentary correspondent, Jonathan Hawker.'

'Right. Cue Jonathan, and take,' the director murmured.

The monitor switched to a head-and-shoulders shot of Hawker in the Westminster studio, looking dramatically into camera.

'Well,' he said breathlessly. 'Quite a sensation in the House tonight. It all began when the Secretary of State for Energy rose to reply to a written question from the member for Southcote East, Morgan Ellis . . .'

The director checked the time. This could mean cutting the piece about the jogging hippo at Bristol Zoo. That chap Brack had gone on a bit, but maybe it was worth it. Hawker knew his job, in any case: he's cut down, no problem.

'. . . Order was not restored,' Hawker was saying, 'until Morgan Ellis applied under standing order nine for an emergency debate on the whole nuclear power programme. Support for this was so strong that the Speaker was obliged to accept it. Next Monday is the most likely date – the day that also sees the opening of the Heathbridge Inquiry.'

The director nodded approvingly as they switched back to the studio. You had to hand it to Jonathan, he was a pro. It looked like they'd have time for the hippo after all.

It was a long time since Harold Harlan had struggled with a champagne cork. One practised twist, and the stuff was bubbling out. Sophie Ferris caught it and handed round glasses to Harlan and Morgan Ellis. Still clutching the bottle, Harlan raised his glass in a toast, every inch the genial host.

'Well, congratulations, Morgan!' he roared.

Sophie took the cue. 'Yes, well done!'

The young MP, flushed with more than just the champagne, clinked his glass with the rest. 'Cheers, and thank you,' he murmured. 'And it must be better than you could've expected!'

Harlan raised one eyebrow as he downed his drink. He was not about to let his pawns take the credit.

'Oh, we all worked pretty hard for it, didn't we, Sophie?' he said with a sly chuckle.

'Not least Paul,' she answered. 'The *Report* had to be the decisive factor. Half the House had copies in their briefcases.'

Ellis smiled knowingly. 'Not including the Right Hon. Minister, I'd guess,' he said. The others laughed, but the MP followed with a hint of criticism. 'Pity Brack couldn't be here. Hamlet without the Prince, don't you think?'

'Oh, Paul's not interested in politics,' Harlan said. 'Or

maybe I should rephrase that. He's not interested in politicians.' The put-down was deliberate. But so was the pickup that followed, as Harlan sighed and after a decent interval allowed himself to be included in the vast tribe of humanity that Paul Brack had no time for. 'Of course,' he added jovially, 'he never believed we could bring this off in the first place. . . .'

Ellis nodded and sipped his drink thoughtfully.

Harlan, however, did not intend to let the party's momentum fade. This was his big day, and no one was going to be allowed to forget it. He brandished the bottle with the relentless generosity of a being from whom all blessings flow, the role he loved.

'Now I've really got something to take to the States and show 'em,' he said. 'Come on. Drink up. We really are on our way at last!'

Angela had insisted on watching the rest of the news, to see if there was anything more about the nuclear issue. There had been the stuff about the emergency debate, which should have pleased Harlan. They had only just switched the set off when the phone rang and Brack picked it up irritably, with an apologetic grimace to his daughter. Probably the Almighty Harold, fresh from the citadels of power, preparing to bend Brack's ear with the tale of how he had Westminster in his pocket. . . .

The caller was not Harlan, however – it was Pat Brack.

'Hello, Paul,' she said quietly. 'I've been trying to ring you.'

'And I've been trying to call *you*,' he answered.

Pat's voice softened. 'A familiar failure of communication.'

God, he was tired. Brack mumbled something noncommittal.

'You seem to have caused quite a stir,' Pat said. Immediately he heard someone else shouting in the room in Oxford: 'She thinks it's brilliant!'

'What's that?'

Pat laughed. 'Just Ollie,' she explained. 'Encouraging me to be forthright in my praise.'

Why did she have to phone tonight? Brack thought. There was so much hard thinking to be done, and maybe some hard actions. 'Pat,' he said haltingly. 'Look, I'm in no great frame of mind just now. I'd like to see you, but . . .'

Out of the corner of his eye he saw Angie rise to her feet and point to the door. She had obviously misread the situation and thought he was hesitating because of her presence.

'No, don't leave,' he said hastily.

Pat's voice again, worried now. 'Paul?'

'It's Angie,' he explained.

'Oh, she's with you?' There was the old edge to her voice, the one that brought out all his guilt. Angela must have come out without telling her, and as usual Pat was the one who had had to do the worrying.

'Oh . . . she popped over to remind me to watch the telly,' he said lamely.

'Good.' The strength had returned to his wife's voice.

'Yes, it was,' Brack said, and he meant it, and not because he had wanted to see himself on the airwaves. He paused, not knowing quite how to put what he was going to have to say next. 'Pat . . .' he began. 'Everyone's telling me to take a holiday now the *Report* is in the can. If I did . . . I'd be very tempted to ask you to come with me.'

'I'd like that.'

'But . . . you see, I don't think that would be right. The point is that I'm tired,' Brack said. 'And I don't want to come . . . courting you in the same self-obsessed state I was in when I left. Do you understand? I need to put my own psyche in order.'

He heard Pat take a deep breath. 'I understand,' she whispered, so softly he could hardly make out the words.

'I'd prefer it, Pat. It *is* necessary. If we're going to give ourselves another chance I don't want it to be a question of picking up where we left off. Pat,' he said quickly, 'I want it to be a new beginning.'

His wife said nothing. Angela was still standing by the door looking at him, not happy, but somehow hopeful. She was old enough now to realize that love – and hope – were very complicated things.

4

Sarah Challen paid little attention at first to the noises downstairs. Maybe it was just Brian getting himself some early-morning tea, she thought sleepily. Then she remembered that the man who had been her research supervisor and was now her lover was supposed to be up in Scotland visiting the Dounreay reactor. She had slept alone last night, and here she was, stark naked in her bed at the crack of dawn with someone banging around in the kitchen. . . .

Sarah shook her head, suddenly totally awake, and threw back the covers. She swung her long, well-shaped legs over the side of the bed and reached for the dressing-gown draped over the bedroom chair, then padded quietly out onto the landing and down the stairs.

The 'intruder' was, in fact, Brian – though what on earth she would have done if it hadn't been him Sarah had not the faintest idea. Screamed and gone for the carving knife? She was not the kind of woman who was easily intimidated, and staying in bed, cowering under the blankets, simply had not occurred to her. She stood silently in the doorway for a long moment, watching Brian Fletcher as he busied himself making tea and toast. The clothes he was wearing had a crumpled look, as if he had been up all night, and his pleasant, even features were pale with lack of sleep. But he was humming to himself, working quickly, almost frantically. If she hadn't known the man better, Sarah would have assumed he was high on something chemical.

He still hadn't noticed her appearance. Sarah smiled to

herself. 'I didn't know you were in the house . . .' she announced loudly.

'God!' Brian jumped back from the kettle, spilling the cup of tea he had just made on to the tiled floor. He looked at Sarah as she padded over, then back at the puddle at his feet, like a small boy who has made an awful mess of some adult task he had desperately been trying to master.

'Sorry, darling,' Sarah pouted, taking a step towards him and fixing him with innocent green eyes. 'But you might have been a rapist.'

'Making tea?'

'I think that's the kind of thing they do round here. You get a better class of pervert.'

Fletcher laughed, despite himself. 'I wish you didn't look so hopeful.'

Sarah embraced him and gave him a welcoming kiss. The nice thing about Brian was that he was a lightweight, and easy on the eye. She had got involved with him, as she realized when she bothered to consider the issue, on the rebound. Sarah had been involved with Paul Brack for a time after he had first left his wife, and they had worked together as colleagues again on the Tchenkov debriefing. Then, when Brack had finally severed his connections with the Atomic Energy Authority in protest at the deportation of the Russian fusion expert to America, Brian had been available – and very willing. Fletcher had come with her to the States to continue the work with Tchenkov in his silken prison at Princeton University. Since that time they had worked together at Culham and more or less lived as man and wife, the 'golden couple' of official government fusion research, twin inheritors of Paul Brack's mantle. The relationship made sense. Its single, invisible flaw was the shadow of Brack, their former chief and her former lover. Fletcher looked well placed for success in the AEA: as a scientist he was no high-flier, but he worked hard, was extremely ambitious, and knew how to play the games that led to promotion in the AEA hierarchy. Most of the time Sarah had nothing against that, for she liked success and the lifestyle that went with it, but there was another side to her, perhaps her legacy from her father, Maxwell Challen. In moving from Brack to Fletcher, Sarah had moved from the supreme idealist to the careerist *par excellence* – perhaps because each mirrored aspects of her own character and motivation . . . contradictions that were still largely unresolved. . . .

'So, what gives?' she said. 'I thought you were in Dounreay for a while yet.'

Fletcher had been waiting for her to ask that. 'Flew down yesterday evening,' he said. 'At Norman Phillips's express request. Thought it was too late to wake you by the time I got here.'

'Thanks,' Sarah said as he handed her a cup of tea. He was obviously relishing the implications of what he had told her. Brian was beginning to leave the ranks of the research scientists and enter the exalted executive bracket, and the change gave him pleasure – perhaps too much.

She watched him put bread in the toaster, then followed him through to the living-room, sipping at her tea as she went. The table was covered in sheets of paper and scribbled notes. Brian picked up a new-looking book.

'Anyway,' he announced. 'I've been up all night. Reading this.'

'Ah . . .' Sarah said, recognizing *The Brack Report*. She was beginning to realize why he had hurried down from Scotland.

'You've seen it?' he asked.

'I read it yesterday.'

'Were you asked to?' he said with visible surprise.

'No.' Sarah tried to sound casual, but she could feel her hackles rising at Fletcher's tone. 'I bought a copy for my personal interest. Okay?'

Fletcher ignored the edge of aggression in her voice. 'So, what do you think?'

Sarah looked at him levelly. 'It's brilliant.'

For a moment he looked disconcerted, then the confusion changed to anger. 'Oh,' he rasped. 'In what way?'

'Darling,' she said with a weary sigh. 'That's a long story. You may have been up all night, but I've only just woken.'

That seemed to make it worse. 'It's unforgivable in my opinion,' Fletcher said. He brandished the book as if it were a piece of outrageous pornography. 'What Brack's done. Here.'

The toaster had popped up. Fletcher hurled the book onto the sofa and stomped out. As he spread his toast in the kitchen, he continued to harangue her.

'For a man like that to turn round suddenly in praise of windmills, cowshit and compost is also pretty bloody ridiculous, don't you think?'

'I must say that's not quite the level on which I read it,' Sarah answered softly.

Brian hadn't heard her – or hadn't wanted to – because when he came back into the room he was launched into a monologue that brooked no argument.

'So the thermal reactors did come out of the nuclear ark,' he spluttered, his mouth full of toast. 'So the advanced gas-cooled reactors may be a bureaucratic and industrial disaster. The pressurized water reactor may not be particularly well-designed from the safety point of view. But they're stages in development,' he said earnestly. 'We learn from them. And the fact is that the Fast Reactor is the only means we in the West have of averting energy starvation.'

Fletcher started on another piece of his breakfast, and Sarah took the opportunity to get a word in. It might be early in the morning, but she suddenly didn't feel like taking this kind of arrogance lying down. She had never particularly admired Brian's scientific brain – his appeal lay in rather different areas – and had always viewed him as a competent journeyman rather than an original thinker. It was time he realized that she could think, too.

'Maybe you decided to skip the section on alternatives, because you thought they'd be concerned only with cowshit and compost?' she said acidly. 'Well, I read that part and I can tell you that you're wrong, Brian. Rhetorical distortions are no match for the arguments in that book.

There is a case against nuclear power, and its power is formidable because it comes from a highly scientific but completely original mind. You ignore that fact at your peril.'

Fletcher had turned pink with anger. 'So that's it, is it?' he snapped. 'Uncle Paul can do no wrong. . . .'

The extreme vehemence was unexpected, though Sarah had been aware that she was raking the embers of old jealousy. Brian's anger had very little to do with intellectual differences, a lot to do with personal resentments. She made one final attempt to be reasonable.

'Brian,' she said as gently as she could, 'it seems to have escaped your notice that the most powerful and scientifically impressive argument in the whole book is his case for *fusion*. You and I believe in it, too.'

Fletcher finished his last piece of toast and looked at his watch. 'So why didn't he stay to work with us at Culham?' he said triumphantly. 'Why couldn't he accept that the nuclear option is the only viable one at the moment and work to make fusion a reality over the next couple of decades?' Sarah tried to speak, but he swept on. 'I'll tell you why,' Fletcher growled angrily. 'Because the man's insane – well, we've known that for a long time. He's a professional outsider, a wrecker. Just look at what he did to Eric Fulton's career over the Wintersham business.'

Sarah waited for him to burn himself out. 'You appear to be in a tearing hurry,' she commented when he had finished. There seemed little else worth saying. The man was absurd, she thought with a new clinical quality that had been creeping into her attitude towards Brian this morning. Yes, he was clumsy. And narrow-minded. Above all, however, stupidly jealous.

Fletcher checked the time again and nodded. He seemed to be calming down. 'Meeting with Norman at eight-thirty. There's a panic on, darling,' he explained. 'Did you hear what happened in the House of Commons last night?'

'Yes. As a matter of fact, I was quite moved by it.'

He reddened again. 'Wait till it moves you out of a job, baby.'

She avoided the jibe. 'So he wants you to prepare some kind of official refutation, does he?'

'Good choice, don't you think?'

The irritating thing was that Brian's statement contained not the slightest element of self-mockery, Sarah thought. 'I think you should read the book more closely,' she retorted stubbornly.

But he was already gulping down his tea, one-handedly scrabbling together his notes and stuffing them into his open briefcase.

'Look, darling,' he said. 'I'm sorry I flew off the handle a bit, but the fact is that it wouldn't be so bad if he hadn't deliberately dropped it into the laps of the anti-nuclear lobby.' He smiled condescendingly. 'There's all kinds of commercial interests casting covetous eyes on *our* funds. They're the pipers who call old Brack's tune, and it doesn't do to forget it.'

Retrieving the copy of *The Brack Report* from beside him on the sofa, he tossed it into the briefcase on top of his notes and reached for his jacket.

'All right, darling,' he said, feeling in his pocket for his car keys. 'See you tonight, maybe. I'll ring you.'

She found herself tolerating his good-bye kiss. A moment later Fletcher was heading for the door, clutching his briefcase, the busy executive eager not to flunk his big chance.

Sarah waited until she heard his car backing out of the drive, then went over to her own briefcase. Her own copy of *The Brack Report* was inside, along with her address book. She leafed through the Report for a few moments, then looked up a number in the address book and began to dial a telephone number with the decisiveness of an action born of impulse.

Sarah Challen had been right to assume that Brack would be up and active, even at this unearthly hour of the morning. He had risen at six, downed the cup of black coffee that usually served him as breakfast, and had been at his desk in the flat before most other people were awake.

He picked up the telephone with a scowl of irritation. He liked to work at home in the early morning because it gave him a couple of hours' grace before the rest of the human race started using the telephone system, and he resented interruptions at this time above all.

'Hello. Brack here,' he growled.

The voice was a woman's, low, pleasant, and familiar.

'Paul. It's Sarah.'

'Of course, Sarah. Ah . . . how are you?' he answered guardedly. He had not seen her for months, and that last time the encounter had been cool, with many things left unsaid on both sides. He had heard she was involved with Brian Fletcher. That had hurt a bit at first, but then Brack had been the one to call off their brief affair, so he couldn't feel he had any claim on her.

'I'm fine, thanks,' he heard he say, although in truth she sounded oddly nervous. Interesting. He had always thought her to be a very self-possessed sort of woman. 'I know you don't like being disturbed this early, Paul,' she continued. 'But . . . actually I just wanted to say how much I liked and admired your book. It . . . well, it all needed to be said by somebody. And I think you've said it brilliantly.'

Brack was bemused to the point of speechlessness. She had been his colleague, his lover. Sarah had always been the one who had tried to keep him involved with fusion at the AEA. He had assumed that she would now be his enemy, along with the rest of them.

'Are you there, Paul?' she asked anxiously.

'Yes, yes. I'm here.'

'But you're not saying anything?'

'I'm . . . well . . . I'm surprised, if you like.'

Sarah laughed, a warm, rich, deep sound, the laugh of a woman confident of her own attraction. There was no ridicule in it, only affection.

'Of course,' she said. 'But I just wanted to let you know

that someone over here in the nuclear stewpot appreciates the shaking-up that you're giving things.'

Brack was still too thrown by the suddenness of it all to say anything coherent, but when she said good-bye and rang off, he sensed something returning to their relationship, perhaps an empathy founded on a new understanding.

He replaced the receiver slowly and leaned back in his chair with a slightly stunned smile. Hearing Sarah's voice again, that throaty laugh and all, had affected him with surprising force. It wasn't so much the sexual reverberations that had touched a nerve – though Sarah was still a very desirable young woman, and there were times when he thought of their times in bed together with a kind of wry longing. No. It was more the shock of the personal meeting the political. Sarah's telephone call raised quite a few questions. Her father, Max Challen, had lost his wife to Norman Phillips as well as being pilloried by the scientific establishment. Sarah's mother and Phillips, Sarah herself and Fletcher – it had all been appallingly neat, and Brack had sometimes wondered whether Sarah would ever show she was her father's daughter. Perhaps that moment had come. She was too bright and too wayward by nature to swallow conventional wisdoms whole like most of the AEA crowd. Brack pushed the emotional implications of the conversation to the back of his mind as best he could. He had promised himself that he would concentrate on mending fences with Pat as best he could, and there was enough work to do in that direction without introducing further complications – Sarah Challen in particular.

Annoyed that one brief conversation could have thrown his mind into such turmoil, Brack decided to go into the office.

After stuffing the papers he would need at work into his briefcase, Brack let himself out of the flat and wandered thoughtfully down the stairs to the gravel courtyard in front of the block, where his bicycle was chained to the railings in its usual spot. He freed the venerable, lovingly maintained machine and set off through the still-silent streets of Waldegrave, encountering a milk float and no more than sprinkling of early-rising workers. He was outside the town, no more than half a mile from his destination, when he was seized by an impulse to delay his arrival a little. Turning off up a winding lane, he clicked the cycle into the lowest of its five gears and rode upwards until he reached a five-barred gate towards the top of a small hill.

The rolling patchwork of the Berkshire countryside lay spread out below him. He had come up to this place several times at week-ends, and it still gave him a frisson of remembered fear. The memory was of the day after the near disaster at Wintersham, when he had cycled up on to a similar hill above the nuclear power station and gazed down to see the station's lights still blazing, the fire engines and police cars crowded beneath the huge dome of the reactor. There had been a leak during experiments with a new refuelling process that he himself had worked on, with several casualties among the station workers. Cracks in the deadly core of the reactor, damage, everyone suspected, from a mild earthquake on the other side of the country. That was all it took.

It was then that he had started to get close to Sarah, perhaps, he pondered as he stood at the gate. He and she had gone into the core area together in the immediate aftermath in their protective suits and then afterwards, around dawn, he had first hinted to her that the time had come for Paul Brack and nuclear power to part company. Two years ago . . . the decision had not been easy, for many reasons, but at least it had been relatively clearcut. The AEA had refused to take his sweeping criticisms of the whole AGR system seriously. And then Harlan had happened along, offering a fat salary and excellent research facilities, another primrose path for the bright lad Brack, one he could persuade himself he believed in. And it couldn't be worse than the AEA. . . .

Well, it hadn't been. He had learnt quite a lot, extended his experience, but working for Harlan International had not been the thrilling challenge he had secretly hoped for. Firstly, a high percentage of the company's efforts seemed to be directed towards devious PR activity – 'creative bullshit', Harlan called it – and what he had learned of Harlan's methods had led him severely to curtail his expectations of the 'alternative energy revolution'. Governments were stubborn and obtuse. As far as the Department of Energy was concerned, the sun still shone out of the AEA's orifice and all was right with the nuclear dream. Nothing was happening, not really happening, and for humanity, as opposed to the proprietor of Harlan International, time was running desperately short.

Brack tore himself away from the view down the valley and got back onto his bicycle. At times like this, a demon voice would whisper to him that he should have stayed with the AEA and worked on fusion, trying to change the system from within instead of breaking free and going for broke. Staying would certainly have helped to keep his marriage together, because Pat seemed to need stability and continuity, and he would have been granted his own budget and research team. A cosy little niche, out of the way. Paul Brack tidied away into a corner of the nuclear bureaucracy and allowed to play with his toys while the dangerous juggernaut of nuclear expansion rolled on. . . . No. He had worked for Harlan, *The Brack Report* had been produced; sooner or later, in this imperfect world, he would fit enough of the pieces together to feel that he had done a real job as a free man and a scientist. Whatever it took.

He freewheeled down the hill and rejoined the main road. Within a few minutes he was at Waldegrave House, where he had worked for the past two years.

The eighteenth-century peer who had built the mansion had conceived of the place as a kind of miniature Versailles crammed into the bosom of Berkshire. Some aristocrats of the time had built grander houses, though not many; others had lost their fortunes on mistresses or at the gambling tables. The Earl of Waldegrave, by one of those reality-defying conjuring tricks for which the English gentry used to be rightly renowned, had managed both to squander his substance and have his palace. The twentieth century, however, had been less kind to his descendants, who had been forced to sell the house at the first whiff of death duties. The white, stucco-fronted pile had become in turn a hotel, a mental hospital, and finally, when the state's resources had also failed to beat the iron laws of accounting, the tax-deductible headquarters and research centre of Harlan International Limited.

Brack could not vouch for Harlan's other vices, but he knew that like the old Earl his employer was a born gambler. The difference was that he believed in calculated risks, and that he made his status symbols work hard for their keep. Where once there had been shady arbors, leisurely walks and baize-smooth lawns, large sections of the grounds had been stripped and put to service. To the right of the drive as Brack cycled up towards the house stood a cluster of experimental windmills. Further on and to the left, squat units of solar reflectors were surrounded by weird vegetation that secreted heaven knew what oils and juices – productive every one, for Waldegrave House was now consecrated to man's search for new sources of energy.

Brack locked his bicycle and walked slowly up the marble steps that swept up to the impressive main entrance of Waldegrave House. Talking to Sarah had brought back memories of another old house – her father's, for it had been there that he had first met Harold Harlan. The project that was to become *The Brack Report* had been taking shape in his mind even then, two years ago, a symptom of the crisis of conscience that had finally taken him away from the AEA. It had also, of course, been the main reason why Harlan had been so eager to snap him up. Brack had no illusions about his employer's motives any more: just a wry curiosity about what Harlan had in mind for him now that the big gun of the Report had been wheeled into action, ready for use in Harlan International's assault on the development budget controlled by the Department of Energy.

There were very few of his colleagues about at this relatively early hour. Dr Scheer, Harlan's American wave-technology adviser, was in the entrance hall. Veejay Patel, in charge of biomass research, greeted Brack cheerfully from the doorway of his lab as Brack made his way along the corridor to his own office. Both men, key members of Harlan's cosmopolitan team, were eager to discuss the Report, but Brack pleaded an important phone call from abroad as an excuse to bolt into his office. The white lies, told to people he respected and had come to consider as friends, seemed even shabbier when he actually made it there. The debris was still all over the place, complete with the copy of the book that he had tossed into the waste bin the previous evening. Nothing had changed. If anything, the chaos looked more dispiriting by daylight.

Brack was still sitting listlessly at his desk, bleakly surveying the cluttered room, when the door was flung open and in strode Harold Harlan, immaculately suited and radiant with positivity and bonhommie.

'G'morning, Paul,' he boomed. 'How's it feel the day after the night before?' He did not wait for an answer. 'Terrific performance on the box last night. Much more like it. What with that and the debate scheduled for Thursday, the aftershock of *The Brack Report* is starting to give a seismic reading on the Richter Scale. What did I tell you?'

Brack nodded but continued to keep his own counsel. Harlan sat himself on the edge of the desk, studiously ignoring the mess all around them. Wait for it, Brack thought: Harlan was catching Concorde to New York today, off to discuss buying a piece of a company that produced aerogenerators – part of his policy of diversifying out of England, just in case things got rough. You could bet even money that he hadn't come all the way down the M4 to hand out medals at this stage, before the campaign had really started to warm up.

Sure enough, the switch from flattery to veiled command came abruptly.

'Just one small thing, Paul,' Harlan continued, still relaxed and friendly. 'I really do want you to take things easy and –' he chuckled '– behave yourself while I'm away in the States. It's only forty-eight hours. Is that too much to ask? You've done everything I hoped for from you, and more. You've put us in a marvellous position. But knowing where to stop is not your strongest point.'

Brack shrugged. 'That's just the problem,' he said. 'I feel as if that's precisely what I've come to. A dead stop.'

'Well, don't fret about that too much,' Harlan answered, patting him on the shoulder. 'No bad thing to ease off and take stock from time to time. I . . . I hesitate to suggest that you go away, because I know how you feel about taking holidays.'

There was a hopeful look on his face which belied his words even as Harlan spoke, but he got no encouragement from Brack.

'Right,' Harlan murmured casually, as if it really didn't matter at all. 'It's your decision. But if you must stay, be content to clean up this mess – looks as though it will take you a good two days – and sit tight. We need some quiet thought about where we go from here, don't you agree?'

'Do you think that *we* go anywhere, Harold?' Brack asked.

'Well, speaking for myself I very much hope so,' Harlan said, looking offended.

'What I mean is: do you have any idea what useful function I might perform in future now that the Report is finished?'

Harlan checked the time, swung himself down off the desk and made his way to the door, nodding emphatically.

'As yet nothing's gone click in my head with the same feeling of absolute rightness I had when I offered you this project which is why I'd like time to reflect, too,' he said. 'You're a valuable man, not to be wasted, and there's plenty of work to be done, no question about that.'

'True. And I don't like being inactive.'

'It won't be for long,' Harlan assured him, looking intently at Brack with every appearance of sincerity. 'Somewhere in all this there's another role waiting to be made by and for you. I trust you about that, Paul, and I need you. So let's just wait on it, and we'll chew everything over properly when I get back.'

'Why not?' Brack answered. His conception of 'chewing it over' was very different from Harlan's, as his boss was well aware. But Harlan let it pass. He had a plane to catch, and he had done the best he could.

When Harlan had gone, Brack continued to sit quietly at his desk, but he no longer felt futile and depressed. The encounter with Harlan had left him with a sense of elation and freedom – precisely the opposite to the effect that had been intended. Perhaps the phone call from Sarah had something to do with it as well, he pondered, a smile forming slowly on his lips as he considered the possibilities. One could chew something over and decide to swallow it. On the other hand, one could also spit it out.

The choice was his, and Brack was beginning to enjoy the prospect of choices.

5

The Dorset countryside was at its best in the mellow light of morning, which was why George Spiking had decided to walk the stretch from the town of Heathbridge to the nuclear site. Spiking, union firebrand and uncrowned monarch of the northern coalfields, liked to see a nice landscape from close up – miners always did, he always proclaimed, what with spending so much time in the muck and the dark. The fresh spring air cleared the mind. Also, it helped keep him calm when he found Barbara Richards, with her feminism and her trendy bedsit Marxism, a pain in the neck. They had both read *The Brack Report*, and now he was being treated by his campaign assistant to a lecture on the 'correct' line of response.

'I can't say I'm exactly disappointed,' she was saying as they walked. 'It's pretty much what I would have expected. . . .'

'Aw, come on, Barby,' Spiking growled, his Yorkshire accent thickening along with his irritation.

Barbara, however, was in mid-flow. 'The facts are there, the arguments are clear, and, yes, it's the best statement of the total case so far. But I was looking for something more,' she explained earnestly. 'I mean, it's got no political perspective at all. There's no attempt to show nuclear power as a symptom of a much deeper disease – as part of the final crisis of capital –'

'Aw, you bloody dogmatists give me the runs,' Spiking cut in impatiently. 'What the hell does all that matter? You heard Brack on the radio, saw him on the telly. Never mind your perspectives: we can use him just the same, don't you see? He's hit the right note at the right time!'

Barbara shot him an enquiring glance. 'What do you mean, we can use him?'

'Put it any way you like. But he's obviously no politician, and if anything that's an advantage,' Spiking said. 'I mean, personally I don't agree wi' a lot of the stuff in Brack's book. This fusion business'd put just as many lads out of work as the nuclear. But even he admits fusion's pie in the sky – and that's better than the reality we've got'

Barbara Richards frowned disapprovingly, which only served to amuse Spiking. Still in his early forties, he had a reputation as a wild man, the union official the popular press loved to hate, but he got results. Ms Richards was hard-working and – most of the time – good company. Without her, TUCANE, the Trade Union Campaign Against Nuclear Energy, wouldn't have got as far as it had. What she didn't understand, though, was the importance of tactics. If she was allowed to have her way they would lose what precarious support they had in the labour movement, which was by no means united on the nuclear issue. And if Spiking often enjoyed his notoriety, he had learned to accept allies and, if necessary, play the moderate where circumstances dictated it.

'Did you read the book's blurb,' she said after a pause. 'About his partner, Harold Harlan?' Spiking seemed, for the moment, to have developed an intense interest in the passing scenery, but she pressed on. 'I'd be careful if I were you,' she said. '"George Spiking in bed with the ex-chairman of a multinational oil company." Imagine what a meal the *Sun* and the *Mail* would make of that!'

Spiking chuckled. He had already been rung up at his hotel in Heathbridge by reporters asking for his reaction to Brack's book. He had been non-committal. No one caught King George exposing his flank, oh no.

'I'm not proposing to sleep with his partner,' he answered. 'There are other ways, love. I wouldn't dream of approaching him directly. But I do think I'll have a little word wi' our friend the Lady Mayor of Heathbridge. She's as much against the site as we are, but no one can tar her with the commie brush. . . .'

His voice trailed off. They were nearing the nuclear site now, and Spiking could see a long column of earth-movers queuing up at the main gate. This was a definite escalation, he thought, and from the number of cars and coaches around it looked as though the police had been specially reinforced for the occasion. He could hear chanting and shouting up by the fence.

'Bloody hell,' Spiking muttered. 'Looks like they're tryin' something on. C'mon, lass.'

Spiking and Barbara Richards broke into a run towards the action. For the moment, tactical fancy footwork was an irrelevancy.

To Brian Fletcher, facing his boss across the polished surface of a very large desk at Harwell, Norman Phillips looked and sounded distinctly tired, despite the trappings of power. Where Fletcher was fresh, keen to meet the challenge, Phillips seemed uneasy and world-weary as he outlined the junior man's brief.

'The truth is that Basil Braintree goofed in the House last night,' he said. 'I tried to warn him, but he's a very conceited man, I'm afraid.' Phillips shrugged. 'Of course when it comes to a debate the whips will be on, so I don't think we need have any real anxiety there. But we do have a problem with *The Brack Report*,' he continued, pursing his lips and tapping against the desk top with the pencil he had been worrying between his fingers during the briefing. 'Did you hear him on the radio?'

Fletcher smiled complacently. 'I certainly did. And my feeling is that if we can keep him talking he'll destroy himself.'

'You're not the first to say that, and you may be right,' Phillips conceded. 'Brack certainly doesn't know the meaning of the word moderation. I thought he overstated his case to the point where it lost credibility.' He looked straight at Fletcher. 'Which is why,' he said deliberately, 'I can't see Harold Harlan allowing him to open his mouth too often in public.'

'I've worked with him, too,' Fletcher said. 'And I'd say that Harlan has no chance in that respect. My bet is that the objectors will try to get hold of him for the Heathbridge Inquiry.'

Phillips grimaced. 'The thought had occurred to me,' he admitted. 'But I had been hoping that *we* could get away with a low profile at Heathbridge. Some of the questions he would be in a position to ask might come uncomfortably close to the knuckle. The public is fickle, as I'm sure you're aware.'

'Exactly,' Fletcher agreed eagerly, leaning forward in his chair. 'So why don't we turn the whole thing to our advantage, take Heathbridge by storm? The objectors will be expecting us to be on the defensive about the AGR. Our strategy should be to play *down* the AGR and go beyond it, to the much bigger issue of our energy future, based on the Fast Reactor.'

Phillips frowned uncertainly. 'The government has already promised an inquiry into the Fast Reactor, as an issue in its own right.'

'Then we take the initiative! We pre-empt it!' Fletcher declared, stabbing the air with his forefinger for emphasis. 'Let's take a leaf out of the French book,' he said. 'I liked the way they announced plans for six new Pressurized Water Reactors the week after the Three-Mile Island scare in the States. Psychologically that's spot on, I'm sure. The best form of defence is attack! Look . . .' he continued, 'what we're promising everyone, when all's said and done, is a domestic energy supply that's virtually limitless and totally independent of any kind of fuel import – *and* of any strike action by the miners. The case for the Fast Reactor can be made in the strongest possible terms, I'm confident of that. And if we can get it across to the broad mass of the public, I'm damned sure they'll buy it.'

Phillips continued to play with the pencil on his desk,

gaining a few seconds' time to think. He was beginning to find Fletcher personally distasteful, but he was also on the brink of giving the young Turk his head. The situation demanded the kind of ruthless, vigorous approach that he was no longer certain he could bring to it. When he had started with the AEA after the war, the public had been complacent, even enthusiastic. There had been the odd voice crying in the wilderness, the likes of Maxwell Challen, but that had been more a social than a political problem. Nevertheless, Fletcher reminded him strongly, even painfully, of his younger self – all arrogant and chipper and raring to show the world, with his eye firmly on the boss's chair. He had done some respectable work on fusion, and he was involved with Sarah, of course – though Fletcher's relationship with Phillips's step-daughter could create as many problems as it had advantages. That said, however, to counter the combination of Brack and Harlan the AEA needed someone with Fletcher's mix of articulacy, push, and devil-take-the-hindmost ambition.

'All right,' Phillips said. 'Prepare along those lines. Our final emphasis will still depend on developments during the next few days, but on the face of things it sounds like an approach that could confound the enemy.'

The hitherto peaceful siege of the Heathbridge nuclear power station site was beginning to turn ugly; not as ugly as Spiking and Barbara Richards had feared at first, but the temperature was clearly rising now that the authorities had brought in the earth-moving equipment. The main gates stood open, and the police had managed to form lines on both sides of the unmetalled road, forcing back the jeering, catcalling protesters to create a narrow corridor for the equipment to enter the site. Just in case, fire hoses had been set up inside the wire, ready to repel any concerted assault as the first of the cumbersome earth-moving machines inched forward towards the perimeter.

George Spiking stood in the roadway between the police lines, chatting easily with Chief Inspector Woods, the officer in charge of site security. Woods, a dry phlegmatic copper of the old school, had been chosen for this job because of his experience in handling demonstrations and industrial disputes, and he and Spiking knew each other of old. There existed a kind of mutual professional respect between the two, even a wary camaraderie. At the moment they were both listening to a woman demonstrator haranguing a fellow activist.

'But what's happening here *is* violence!' she was shouting. 'Thirty thousand people could get killed, just like that! Genetically deformed kids could go on being born for a hundred and fifty years! So why are we being so prissy about violence to bloody machines?'

Woods grimaced and turned away.

'We could do without that kind of talk,' he commented stoically. 'At least your miners are well disciplined, George. This lot are at each other's throats when they're not giving my lads a rough time.'

Spiking answered with a resigned shrug, then decided to go on the offensive. He gestured in the direction of the main gate, still clogged with machinery and seething protesters.

'What I'd like to know is, who the hell let this happen,' he said.

'Start date for the site work's been fixed for weeks,' Woods answered crisply. 'Whatever comes out of the inquiry, George, there's going to be a power station of some sort here. And if it turns out to be coal after all, I should think your boys'll be throwing their hats up.'

Cynical bastard, Spiking thought. He was saved from having to reply by the arrival of a massive articulated truck, picking up speed between the police lines with a hefty bulldozer on its trailer. The union leader stared at it balefully. 'Bloody marvellous sense of timing, I must say, Inspector.'

Barbara Richards emerged from the crowd and drew Spiking away from the inspector.

'I've found Mrs Minchin, George,' she hissed. 'Over with the TV people.'

The pair of them began to fight their way through the crowd to the open ground where the television crews had set up their cameras. The mayor of Heathbridge was giving them her usual good talking-at.

Margaret Minchin, OBE, JP, had always been a faithful Tory, but these days she was becoming a conservationist first and Conservative second. She certainly looked every inch the county lady, from her headscarf and tweeds down to her Derry boots – which was why, against this bizarre background, she made such superb television.

'As mayor of Heathbridge,' she told Nick Rowe, the ITN reporter, 'I don't want any kind of power station here. At least, not on this scale. It has nothing to do with the needs of the area . . .'

'But you're not against nuclear power as such?' Rowe probed smoothly.

Margaret Minchin was unruffled. 'I'm still a "don't know" on that,' she answered with a tinkling laugh. 'I'm not a technical person, and many of the arguments are beyond me. But in this campaign, of course, we've rubbed shoulders with the anti-nuclear people, and I have to admit that I'm more and more impressed by them. Take George Spiking, for example. Before all this blew up I loathed the sight of him, and the idea that we might actually agree about anything would have been laughable. But there are one or two questions we see eye to eye about these days.' She smiled disarmingly into camera, then became serious. 'No, seriously though, I do think the government is being frightfully silly and obstinate on this issue. . . .'

Mrs Minchin could see George Spiking out of the corner of her eye, waving to gain her attention, and she seemed to run out of steam. Rowe had enough footage of the good lady in the can. He called 'Cut!' and thanked her.

'Hello, George,' Mrs Minchin called, stepping over towards Spiking with a genuinely affectionate smile.

Spiking answered with a toothy grin of greeting. 'Hello, Margaret,' he said. He had always been popular with the girls, particularly posh ones who liked a rough diamond.

Dear old Mrs M. was a pushover. 'Not so pretty down here this morning, eh?' he said, jerking a thumb towards the scenes at the gate.

'No. And quite a to-do in the Commons last night. That man Brack sounds very interesting. . . .'

Spiking raised his eyebrows, feigning surprise but in fact hardly able to believe his luck. 'Yes,' he said quickly. 'In fact, now that you mention it I'd been meaning to have a little word with you about that business.'

He put an arm round her shoulder and drew her away from the reporters. At the main gate, the crowd had managed to press the police line forward so that the corridor was too narrow for the artic bearing the bulldozer to proceed any further towards the site gates. Spiking's intense conversation with Mrs Minchin was drowned by a great roar of triumph from the massed protesters.

Pat Brack was running late for collecting Oliver from his dentist's appointment. She drove as quickly as safety allowed through the streets of Oxford, most of them narrow thoroughfares never meant for cars, with her lecturer's gown and briefcase on the passenger seat beside her and the radio tuned into the mid-day news bulletin.

The Brack Report was getting some more media exposure. This time it was Morgan Ellis, the anti-nuclear MP, who was praising the book for its role in precipitating the emergency debate scheduled for later in the week.

'You see, it does just occasionally happen in our creaking democracy that common sense will prevail over party dogma. And one thing I think we can be sure . . .' Pat heard Ellis's self-assured politician's laugh '. . . Basil Braintree will certainly be reading *The Brack Report* in time for Thursday's debate in the House. And that's something gained.'

The news announcer moved on to describe scuffles between police and demonstrators that morning at the Heathbridge nuclear site. Pat listened vaguely as she drove along St Giles's, past the college buildings, heading for the

Banbury Road. She had been lucky to have her teaching job when the troubles with Paul came; at first the work had been a means of helping to pay the bills, but if she was honest with herself she had to recognize that it had been a factor in their estrangement. Teaching had given her independence, something to cling to, and it had also enabled her to meet people who were not obsessive and wayward, but who were rational and civilized, 'normal' in a way that her husband had never been. Well . . . it would be interesting, and quite possibly nerve-racking, to see how Paul reacted to being a media celebrity and a political football.

Pat's Mini drew up outside the Victorian house in North Oxford where the dentist's surgery was. She turned off the radio and beeped the horn. Oliver's face appeared briefly at the waiting-room window, then he was coming down the steps, making for the car. She opened the passenger door for him. He picked up the gown and briefcase and sat down beside her with them on his lap, looking slightly flushed.

'How was it?' Pat asked.

'Not too bad – two fillings, and he took some X-rays,' Oliver said tersely.

She kept talking as they moved back into the stream of traffic. Oliver didn't really seem in the mood, but it helped to keep her mind off Paul.

'And how was Mr Woolley?' They had been visiting the same dentist ever since moving to Oxford, and he had become almost a friend of the family.

'Oh, he was all right,' Oliver said, though Pat noticed that the flush in his face had deepened. 'But he went on a lot about Dad,' he continued. '"Stuck his neck out a bit, don't you think, Ollie?"' he said, mimicking the dentist's fruity baritone voice. 'He seemed to think Dad had done something . . . sort of . . . anti-social.' The boy stopped, torn between family loyalty and embarrassment, noticing that his mother was nodding. 'Well, has he?' he asked uncertainly, suddenly more like a child than a brusque, self-confident adolescent.

Pat gritted her teeth. 'Your father's neck is permanently at full stretch. That's what makes him impossible to live with.'

'"Made" or "makes"?' Oliver asked sharply.

She glanced at him and realized she must be showing the strain, because Oliver looked quickly down at the gown in his lap and changed the subject. 'How was the – er – lecture?' he said.

'Oh, the usual. Okay,' Pat murmured, grateful to be let off the hook and wishing there was some way you could explain to a sixteen-year-old that you could love a man and still be unable to live with him – for the moment.

Brack was barely on time at the restaurant. If it hadn't been for his secretary's reminder, he might still have been sitting in the office instead of being here, seated opposite the delightful Sophie Ferris, surrounded by the expense-account aristocracy and about to embark on a meal that would cost about as much as he usually spent on food in a month.

'. . . With sauté potatoes, broccoli spears, and . . .' Sophie glanced away from the waiter to Brack. 'Glazed carrots?' she asked.

Brack nodded wryly. 'Fine. Fine. . .' This was her scene, not his.

'And we'll have a bottle of the Givry-Chambertin, number twenty-eight,' she said, rounding off the order. The waiter nodded and whisked away the menus without sparing a glance for her male companion.

'Well, Sophie,' Brack began, settling back in his wicker chair. 'This is very pleasant. I'd be flattered, except that I imagine it's also part of a Harold injunction to keep me out of mischief.'

'No comment,' Sophie said with a teasing laugh. 'Though obviously we're all concerned that you don't feel played out. Post-creative depression and all that. Had any ideas about your next move?' she added, taking a sip of her campari and soda.

Brack chuckled inwardly. So a woman fifteen years younger than himself had been dispatched to keep a motherly eye on him. Ho-hum. 'Actually,' he said, fighting hard to keep a straight face. 'I've decided to follow everyone's advice. I intend to spend a few days at the seaside.'

'Oh, I'm glad,' Sophie said brightly. Then came a touch of uncertainty. There was something ominously mischievious in Brack's dead-pan expression. 'Have you . . . thought where you'd like to go?'

'Weymouth.'

That was all she needed to know. 'I see,' Sophie said, the girlish enthusiasm gone. 'And I don't suppose you'll be doing much in the way of paddling . . .'

Brack nodded. 'I shall have to commute. There's a shortage of hotel rooms in Heathbridge, what with the Inquiry opening next week.'

Sophie's smile was very uneasy now. She delved quickly into her handbag and produced an envelope.

'Compliments to the chief,' she explained. 'I don't suppose you'll want to change your mind, but Harold suggested I offer you these – just in case you were undecided.'

Brack let out a long-suffering sigh and examined the envelope's contents – two first-class air tickets and an open-ended hotel booking for Mauritius.

'They say it's particularly lovely at this time of year,' Sophie said.

Brack smiled broadly. 'You sound hopeful. Were you thinking of joining me?'

'I think I'd be licensed to do almost anything to keep you away from the Heathbridge Inquiry,' Sophie answered, fluttering her eyelashes.

They both laughed, but Brack tossed the tickets back on the table. 'I'm just going to meet people,' he said, still smiling but with a firmness that signalled an end to the shadow-boxing.

The waiter arrived with the wine, automatically offering it to Brack for approval.

'I trust the lady's judgement,' he said. When the waiter, nodding indulgently, insisted on pouring some into a glass for Brack to taste, he pushed it away. 'I also rely on her taste.'

Sophie held out her own glass. The waiter, rather put out, eventually poured and accepted her approving nod. The little charade over, Sophie looked searchingly at Brack.

'Did someone invite you?' she asked.

'The mayor of Heathbridge,' Brack said. 'A very charming lady – and one totally without ambition to control me, I should judge.'

Sophie ignored the chiding in his tone. 'Don't be so sure,' she said, quickly returning to the attack. 'Paul, you're the man they've been hoping for. They'll use you, abuse you – they won't care about your future.'

'If you think I've got one of those, I'd be glad to hear of it,' Brack shot back, and for the first time there was a hint of bitterness in his voice.

'Look, Paul,' Sophie pleaded. '*The Brack Report* has put us right in the centre of the energy policymaking stage. Heathbridge is only . . . peripheral. . . .'

'You think so? I'm not sure the powers-that-be would agree with you.' He shrugged. 'Anyway, I thought I'd just go and find out.'

Sophie shook her head. 'Don't jeaopardize all you've achieved, Paul. And I'm not being Harold's messenger-girl when I say that. That's my personal worry.'

Brack waved one hand, dismissing her fears, personal or otherwise, for his well-being.

'So tell me, what *have* I achieved?' he asked. 'The Report may have raised the dust a little, and for all I know may continue to do so. But the implications of it require change, decision, commitment, sacrifice, hard work. Those things mean no easy options – and therefore a hell of a lot of electoral unpopularity. Morgan Ellis will soon find that out. Certainly he's aroused a flutter of support on the back benches, where they're always eager for a bit of harmless controversy, but you wait – soon the next "cause" will come along, and they'll all roll over and go back to sleep.'

'And I thought Harold was the cynic round here, Paul Brack!' Sophie said. 'He thinks your book is solid gold. To hear him, you'd believe it was about to move mountains.'

'He didn't mix his metaphors quite so outrageously,' Brack commented. 'But yes, to hear him talk that's roughly the impression. Do you think he's serious?' he asked, suddenly returning to the attack.

Sophie smiled. 'That's a leading question. And the answer is in the positive. It's the best thing he's managed to get into his well-manicured hands for a long time, and you know it. Are you looking for flattery from me?'

'Oh, this lunch invitation is flattery enough, Sophie.'

'But not necessarily a guarantee that Paul will be a good boy?'

'No.'

Sophie nodded glumly. 'And that's what I tell Harold. . . . He'll be delighted.'

Brack decided to relax the pressure. Their main course was arriving, and he didn't want to spoil the poor girl's lunch entirely.

'Don't worry too much,' he coaxed. 'I may even be back here before Harold is. And it's not beyond the bounds of possibility that I might fall asleep just as soundly as our honourable members,' he added with an impish grin. 'In a deckchair on Weymouth beach.'

6

Mrs Minchin locked the door of her unpretentious saloon.

'This is St Andrew's Church Hall,' she said, pointing to the drab building on the other side of the car park. 'The Co-Ordinating Committee's already here, so you'll be able to meet everybody.'

Brack, tired from his hurried train journey, stared unenthusiastically through the dusk and nodded. 'Fine,' he said.

'Some of the groups are so much on the fringe that we simply haven't been able to embrace them all,' the mayor continued. During their trip from the station she had become rather used to making the conversational running with this unexpectedly reticent scientist. 'However, I think we have achieved a degree of consensus amongst the most powerful voices. And since everyone speaks so favourably about your book, I thought that might be a kind of standard to which all the disparate elements could rally.'

Brack's eye was caught by a handbill pasted to the wall which read: 'SMASH THE SYSTEM MEANS NUKES OUT'. Disparate elements was right. He rather liked Mrs Minchin, but he wasn't about to rush into any commitments.

'This is TUCANE's HQ, actually,' she was saying. 'That's George Spiking's trade union organization. Have you met him?'

Brack shook his head. 'No, but I've read quite a lot.'

'Ah,' said Mrs Minchin, then continued quickly, 'Well, he's been very active here for the past week or so. We're poles apart politically, of course, but by golly I have to admire his organizing ability. No wonder the trade unions have the country by the throat!'

The tinkling Minchin laugh followed. She took his arm as they arrived at the door of the hall, restraining him while she explained the niceties.

'Each evening we've tried to bring together members of the different groups. Part business, part social. And a different venue each night – so no one feels slighted,' she added with a disapproving smile. 'It's astonishing how sensitive people are.'

Brack agreed, but he did not share her apprehension. Mrs Minchin, he guessed, was probably used to cosy Tory committees and Chamber of Commerce jovial unanimity, which was why she found some of her new allies hard to understand. Personally, he had always thrived on controversy, and this would add spice to an interesting expedition.

'Thanks for the preamble,' he said. 'Shall we go in?'

In fact, the atmosphere at the church hall was more like a small, low-key cocktail party than a gathering of sectarian campaigners. The representatives were a very mixed bunch, with a strong leavening of country worthies who would normally have shunned anything that smacked of protest. Brack was quickly introduced to several county councillors, a lady from the Town and Country Planning Association, and finally to George Spiking himself. Contrary to what some of his colleagues might say, Paul Brack could be a good listener – when he was at the learning stage. At the moment he felt he could gain something by hearing what the activists and political campaigners had to say. He was impressed by George Spiking's rough, almost brutal vitality, and while he personally felt no draw towards the man's politics, or his limited view of the energy problem, he knew instinctively that here was a gifted organizer. Spiking would use him if he could – and if Brack didn't use him first.

'By writing that book you've really thrown your hat into

the ring,' Spiking told him. 'At a time like this, no one can hide in his study.'

Brack smiled. 'Oh, I'll listen to the way you plan to do things. If there's any way I can think of helping, I'll let you know.'

'Good. We need experts,' Spiking said. He lowered his voice. 'It's all either gentry, worried about the local amenities, or the woolly-hat and Morris Traveller brigade,' he whispered with a conspiratorial grin. 'You're a man with an overall view, a scientist's view. People'll take notice. . . .'

Mrs Minchin appeared, took Brack by the arm and led him away to meet a Young Liberal or two. Spiking watched contentedly. He reckoned he'd got the fish hooked, and it promised to be a fat catch, though he knew that he and everyone else would have to be ready for one or two surprises. Brack was shrewd: all reticent charm until he found his feet and had a reason to disagree with you, at which time you'd realize he could be hell to deal with. It would, in fact, take a George Spiking to handle him.

Spiking's opinion of Brack was reinforced during the formal meeting that followed. The odd quiet word from Brack, the occasional point of information, broke many a stalemate. By the time, close to midnight, that Mrs Minchin, as chairman, decided they should bring the talking to a close, they had agreed substantively on an approach to the presentation of evidence. With just over forty-eight hours to go before the inquiry opened, agreement was becoming a pressing necessity. Mrs Minchin was delighted.

'My goodness,' she said, with a weary smile. 'If anyone had suggested that we'd have ironed out our problems and agreed the order in which evidence should be presented, I'd never have believed them. And we've achieved it amicably, too,' she added comfortably, replacing the cap of her fountain pen with a decisive flourish. Then she saw Paul Brack trying to catch her eye, and acknowledged his desire to speak despite the lateness of the hour.

'Apart from expressing an ingrained mistrust of any

agreement that can be described as amicable,' Brack said sardonically, 'I do in fact have a bit to say. May I?'

'Please.'

Brack leaned back in his rickety canvas-backed chair and pursed his lips thoughtfully.

'It has become the tendency at inquiries of this kind,' he began, 'for the inspector to take the attitude that the applicants are innocent until proved guilty, so to speak. Now in a criminal court that's fair enough, because the onus is on the police to prove guilt, and they're a full-time professional organization whose job it is to do just that. But in this kind of inquiry you, the objectors, are unpaid volunteers. You claim no expenses and you have to beg for cut-price professional help. I hope, by the way, that you don't take that as a personal criticism, because it isn't meant like that.' He paused and looked around the large table. No one gainsaid him, and he continued. 'You see, in comparison with the massive weight of the Central Electricity Generating Board, the United Kingdom Atomic Energy Authority, and their sponsors, the Department of Energy, you are neither strong nor, ultimately, united in purpose.'

One or two faces reddened slightly. Other members of the committee studied their notes intently. But they carried on listening, waiting for this man, who had burst on them like some quietly relentless *deus ex machina*, to make his revelation.

'As I understand the procedure, the applicants will open with a statement of their case. It will be clear-cut, massively researched, and closely argued by a single voice. You, too, will have the right to make opening statements. But that right may not be used as effectively as you would like. The gist of all your various cases as I've heard them tonight is negative. That's not your fault,' Brack said hastily. 'You are attacking the nuclear position, which has become established public policy. Nevertheless, that negative quality does put you at a disadvantage: everyone believes there is an energy crisis, and yet you are proposing that we deny ourselves the nuclear option. Full stop. An invidious position . . .'

Spiking, following Brack's arguments from several places to his right, turned quietly to Barbara Richards and gave her a huge wink. 'I think he's taking the bait,' he whispered.

Brack, meanwhile, was moving towards his conclusion.

'What seems to be lacking from the evidence I've heard outlined,' he commented, 'is the statement of a strong, positive, alternative case. One which not only meets but actually surpasses the social and economic objectives of the CEGB's plan. To sum up: I think you must force the tribunal into a position where they have not merely to consider your objections but also to assess two viable alternatives and be seen to decide between them.'

Spiking was nodding enthusiastically. Brack smiled at him.

'If that makes any sense to you, I'm happy,' he said. 'And unless you have anyone else in mind, I think I'm the obvious person to make that case.'

'Hear! Hear!' Mrs Minchin responded, beaming with pleasure.

Brack acknowledged the wave of applause from the committee members and looked at his watch. It was a quarter after midnight: Harold Harlan would be back from the States in about twelve hours, which gave him just that time until all hell broke loose. The whole affair had a sense of inevitability about it – Harlan and Sophie had been right about that. But at this moment Paul Brack felt cleansed, true to himself in a way he had almost forgotten during the long years in the nuclear industry and even with Harlan International. He had a chance to use his knowledge directly, and he had choices.

The expensively dressed, confident-looking man who made his way through the barrier and out into the Concorde terminal at Heathrow Airport at noon the next day was not aware of Paul Brack's choices – yet. Overnight bag in one hand, gleaming attaché case in the other, Harold Harlan had returned from his lightning trip to New York to find his Rolls-Royce and Sophie Ferris waiting and, as far as he knew, all right with the world. Sophie, however, lost no time. She was carrying a copy of the *Sun*, folded to the appropriate page.

'Welcome, Harold dear,' she said, thrusting the paper at him. 'You can read the facts in the rest of the press, but maybe this will do for easy digestion.'

Harlan looked down at the page. 'REBEL ATOM SCIENTIST TO LEAD ATTACK ON NUKE PLAN', the headline read. Beside it was a picture of an intense-looking Brack at his press conference at Waldegrave House. The photograph was blotchy, but of all things the sign behind Brack saying 'Harlan International' was easily legible.

Harlan winced momentarily, but he had a swift recovery rate. He took the paper, folded it under his arm and called for his chauffeur to put his bags in the Rolls.

'Got your own car?' he rasped. Sophie nodded. 'Okay, Sophie. You did right to tell me. You'd better get back and hold the fort. No comment if anyone rings, all right?'

'See you later then?' Sophie said.

'If I don't get arrested for wringing the stupid bastard's neck!'

Harlan strode over to the open door of the Rolls, eased himself into the back seat and slammed the door. A second later the car swept away from the terminal building, leaving Sophie Ferris forlorn on the pavement. Harold Harlan, true to form, had found some trouble – and he was about to shoot it.

'It will be my intention,' Brack said, 'to draw the Tribunal's attention to the fact that there *are* alternatives to nuclear power – alternatives that are not tainted with horrifying military implications, and which require no cloak of secrecy to keep them from prying public eyes. My own preference is the fusion process, as opposed to nuclear fission, as a safer method, and one which does not need expensive raw materials from world flashpoints such as Namibia. I will argue that the chemical process itself is well known, and that the technology required is not a far-off dream but would be achievable if a mere fraction of the billions of pounds being poured into nuclear technology were to be made available. I have a good deal of experience in the field, which I am prepared to use openly, whether the powers-that-be like it or not.'

As Brack spoke, a helper slipped quietly into the meeting-room and tip-toed over to Margaret Minchin. After a whispered conversation, the helper made her way over to Brack. He paused, listened, then nodded.

'I'm afraid something's come up,' he announced with a sour smile. 'Perhaps you'd like to take a break while I sort it out. A professional problem . . .'

'Then we'll have a cup of tea while we wait for you,' Mrs Minchin said.

Brack stood up. 'An excellent idea. I'll join you as soon as I've solved my little local difficulty.'

Harold Harlan was waiting outside the hall beside the parked Rolls, arms folded and radiating pent-up aggression.

'Ah, Harold,' Brack said cheerfully when he caught sight of him. 'I thought I had another hour's grace. I suspect you whistled down the M3 without a thought for speed limits.'

Harlan, stony-faced, said nothing.

'You must be here for a fight,' Brack continued. 'Or . . .?'

'I just want to know what the hell you think you're up to,' Harlan growled finally.

Brack's smile turned into a laugh.

'Don't laugh at me!' Harlan bellowed. He opened the car door. 'Get in.'

Brack shook his head, still grinning. 'No,' he said. 'I want neutral ground.'

Harlan sighed in furious exasperation. 'Look, this is serious, Paul,' he said heavily.

'Then why have you lost your sense of humour? It's useful at times like these – and I don't trust you when you're wild.'

'All right,' Harlan conceded, slamming the door to and thrusting his hands in the pocket of his jacket. 'Where do you want to go?'

'For a walk.'

Harlan set off reluctantly behind Brack, who was already moving down the quiet back street. 'Paul,' he pleaded, walking quickly to catch up. 'Do you realize that you're endangering billions of dollars of potential investment?' When he arrived alongside Brack, he took him by the arm. 'This inquiry here's just window-dressing,' he said urgently. 'Nothing that happens here is going to change government policy. It's the classic process. Justice has to *seem* to be done.'

Brack turned on his heel, stopping him short. 'We're better off lobbying MPs and buying them expensive lunches, are we?' he shot back.

'For Christ's sake, Paul, we've got ourselves an emergency debate!'

'And this time the whips will be on,' Brack scoffed. 'They'll get their regular majority, whatever the force of the argument. It's window-dressing, too, Harold. Just a big upmarket, that's all.'

The barb hit home. Harlan became defensive.

'All right, all right,' he said. 'I'll do without your help. But I do want you to keep out of my way.' He paused, and when he continued there was an edge of desperation in his voice. 'I had time to read the papers on the way down here, Paul, and some of them had managed to get a picture of you with George Spiking, of all people. That's what worries me!'

They were walking again now. Brack stared at the pavement. 'I was invited to come here, Harold,' he said simply. 'Originally I'd intended just to meet people and maybe offer some advice, but since then I've found kids who are prepared to go to prison, and more! *This* is the battleground, don't you see? People are frightened, as I remember you telling me not so long ago when it suited your argument. I know better than most that they have darned good reason to be. Here, at last, I have the opportunity to do more than simply sit on the sidelines and fire off salvoes with my typewriter.'

They had recrossed the street and were back within a few yards of the entrance to the hall. Harlan stood listening to Brack, gazing with open loathing at the shabby little building and flurry of clumsily printed posters outside. Here he was among the do-gooders, the idealists, the muddle-heads. The losers. He, Harold Harlan, was a money-grubbing, vain, luxury-loving, ruthless sort of bastard, but couldn't Brack have the sense to see that he would achieve more, in the final analysis, than these earnest dreamers?

Harlan waited patiently for him to finish his speech before he made his final pitch.

'Paul,' he said, laying one hand on his shoulder. 'You put four years into *The Brack Report*, and it's dynamite. If your puritan upbringing has to rear its ugly head, let it rest on that. You've done your bit – and it's more significant than anything you can achieve here.'

Brack, however, was already becoming restless. If he was going to get things straight before the inquiry opened, he dare not waste time. There was a touch of sadness as well as defiance in the way he smiled at Harlan.

'Oh, that was the preaching, Harold,' he said, half turning towards the door. 'Now I have to practise.'

Sarah Challen was in the kitchen of her flat, unpacking her shopping, when she heard a key turn in the outside door. There were times when she wished she hadn't granted Brian the key, and this was one of them. She had been hoping for a chance to think before he turned up home. He was in the hall now, calling out a greeting, but she carried on dourly with her task. Brian had a certain unnervingly zestful way of shutting that damned front door when he had had a good day. Increasingly she found herself wishing he'd just have a really rotten day for once.

Sure enough, he swept in wearing a jaunty grin. Sarah was packing salad vegetables into the crisper box of the fridge, so she was shielded from the initial impact of his entrance. It didn't last long: she scarcely managed to utter a reasonably civil 'hello' before he hauled her up and spun her into his arms, ignoring the fact that her hands were still full of tomatoes.

'So, how's your day been?' Brian Fletcher enthused, oblivious of the fact that anything might be wrong. As usual, he didn't wait for an answer, which in this case was a relief. Within moments he was heading through into the living room to fix them both drinks.

Sarah stayed standing in the middle of the tiled kitchen floor, bracing herself to deliver the message she had been brooding over for the past quarter of an hour.

'Norman's office at Harwell phoned fifteen minutes ago,' she called out, making a face at her own reflection in the kitchen cabinet. 'They want you to ring back as soon as possible.'

Fletcher appeared in the doorway immediately, eager and enquiring.

'Anything to do with Heathbridge?'

Sarah winced inwardly. He was about to do battle with a former colleague, and he was going to enjoy every second.

'Yes,' she said quietly. 'Apparently they do have some intelligence – that was the word they used – about Paul. He *is* going to be at Heathbridge. There's some indication that he's not only going to be principal witness but that he might even open the objectors' case for them.'

She could see Fletcher savouring the information. He shook his head slowly in delighted disbelief, and he smiled – like a hunter who has seen some long-sought quarry wander carelessly into the sights of his gun.

'But . . . that's marvellous news, darling,' he said at last. 'Every time the man opens his mouth, we score points! He's a walking PR disaster area!'

Sarah looked at him icily. 'I'm not sure you have any rational basis for that assumption,' she murmured. 'You never won an argument with Paul in the old days, and I don't see you starting to get an advantage now.'

But Fletcher simply grinned more broadly. Sarah's lingering attachment to Brack was a lovable weakness. The man was a hopeless case, chasing frantically after his own tail, a latter-day version of Sarah's own father – and everyone knew where his dissident visions had got old man Challen.

'Oh, come on,' he chided her. Not that he could really be angry with Sarah, not now. Brian Fletcher turned back into the living room, homing in on the telephone, ready to commune with Norman Phillips and his own bright new destiny.

7

The official inquiry into the application of the Central Electricity Generating Board to construct a nuclear power station on the site near Heathbridge opened on Thursday morning, in the workaday surroundings of a comprehensive school hall on the outskirts of the town. The Planning Tribunal, chaired by the Hon. Justice Wilkinson, QC, sat on a raised dais at the end of the room, with 'applicants' to the right and 'objectors' to the left. Public, witnesses and press were separated on to rows of uncomfortable chairs in the cavernous main body of the hall.

The opening day saw the inquiry well attended. Both sides had brought up their big guns for the start. Bill Murphy, chairman of the CEGB, sat with Norman Phillips, surrounded by a full team of technical advisers and expert witnesses, among them Brian Fletcher, who was seated strategically just behind Phillips, ready for the call. The objectors – including counsel for Friends of the Earth, the Town and Country Planning Association, the Council for the Preservation of Rural England, plus Mrs Minchin as mayor of Heathbridge and George Spiking on behalf of TUCANE – were distinctly thinner on the ground and less monolithic in appearance. At the moment, however, they held the limelight through the efforts of Paul Brack. True to form, he had launched straight into an attack on the credentials of one of the tribunal's members, the eminent scientist Sir Frank Dutton.

Justice Wilkinson had a reputation in legal circles for being a comparatively liberal judge, though a stickler for procedure, and he peered at Brack disapprovingly over the tops of his half-moon spectacles. His expression seemed to say: Good Lord, man, this is a planning application, not an episode of 'Perry Mason'. But Brack, hands in pockets and casually combative, clearly relished the role he had decided to assume.

'But Sir Frank is a member of the National Radiological Protection Board, sir,' he declared. 'This is an organization which for some time has been campaigning to have internationally permissible level of radiation not lowered, but raised. As you will know, sir, the nuclear industry in this country is in the habit of sluicing much of its low-level radioactive wastes into the Irish Sea, and we shall be producing a considerable body of evidence to show that, so far from being raised, those radiation limits need to be drastically reduced. In that context, sir, I hope you will agree that Sir Frank must be regarded as a hostile witness.'

Justice Wilkinson leaned forward slightly, and his stare became colder. 'Sir Frank Dutton is not a witness, Dr Brack, but an assessor,' he told Brack with studied politeness.

Brack smiled. 'A mere Freudian slip, sir,' he rejoindered, unabashed. 'It is in his capacity as an assessor, of course, that I raise my objection to him.'

There were subdued titters from among the general public, and in the press section journalists exchanged knowing smiles. Brack looked as though he was going to be good value, just as they had hoped. After all, these bloody inquiries were usually all piss and wind. Here was one where they might get some red meat.

'But before you rule on that, or whatever it is you do,' Brack continued, 'I'd like to raise one other objection to the composition of the tribunal. In presenting our case we intend not only to discredit that of the applicants but also, lest you should be prejudiced with the thought that we are merely a destructive element, to present an alternative non-nuclear plan to supply the energy needs which the Electricity Board claims to have identified.'

At the applicants' table Bill Murphy raised an eyebrow at his neighbour, Norman Phillips. The representative of the UKAEA did his best to look unconcerned, but behind them Brian Fletcher quietly pursed his lips and started to scribble notes. He had been right: this was going to be just the battle he had predicted.

'In doing so,' Brack said. 'We shall be giving evidence of the so-called 'soft technologies'. At Windscale much expert evidence was adduced in this area but was, however, ignored in the final report.' He looked directly at Justice Wilkinson. 'It would, of course, be quite improper to think that such information was deliberately ignored,' he said carefully. 'It is much more likely that the tribunal was simply incompetent to assess the merits of the evidence. . . .'

That brought reaction from his own side. George Spiking covered up a grin, but allowed himself an inward chuckle of admiration. Mrs Minchin shifted nervously in her seat, beginning to wonder quite what she had done in bringing this spoiler into the contest.

Brack wound up his opening remarks. 'But,' he suggested, 'in order to prevent such a catastrophe – I use the word advisedly – from occurring again, perhaps it would be prudent to co-opt on to the tribunal an assessor who will have some inkling of what our witnesses will be talking about.'

He sat down without further ado, to murmurs and some irreverent laughter from the body of the hall. Justice Wilkinson took off his spectacles and cupped his chin in his hands.

'I must say that I find the tone of your remarks somewhat offensive, Dr Brack,' he drawled ominously.

Brack was back on his feet immediately.

'It's a problem that has beset me for most of my professional life, sir,' he said. 'However, if you could concentrate your attention on the content of what I say rather than the tone in which I say it, I think the vital purpose of this inquiry will be better served.'

Justice Wilkinson blinked in astonishment, but decided to save further strictures for when they were really needed, which they most assuredly would be at this rate. He missed the majesty of the Bench on these occasions: the trouble was that there was no such offence as contempt of inquiry.

The arguments about the fitness of the assessors dragged on until the lunch adjournment. Participants and public emerged into the playground to find TV news cameras set up outside the door.

Sarah Challen waited beside her car, surveying the mêlée with jaundiced disinterest. Then she saw Pat Brack, standing waiting like her, but by the main door. Sarah felt a surge of jealousy within her which surprised her conscious mind with its force. She had thought the brief flurry with Paul after he left the authority was done with. Perhaps it had to do with the fact that Pat looked very different from what she would have expected: calm, attractive, strong. Whatever she was going through, she knew how to hide it, Sarah thought – which was more than she could say about her relationship with Brian.

Fletcher was striding across the asphalt of the playground now, but Sarah continued to gaze at Pat. Suddenly the other woman turned, and their eyes met across a hundred yards. Sarah forced a smile, knowing it must look guilty. It was not returned. Calm, be damned . . .

Fletcher arrived in time to witness the moment. He turned and looked in Pat Brack's direction, then at Sarah.

'God, what an insufferable man Brack is,' he muttered, steering her towards the car.

Sarah wasn't sure whether he was referring to Brack's relationship with his wife or his behaviour at the inquiry that morning. Probably both: when Brian hated, he did not discriminate.

'Where would you like to go for lunch?' she said tersely, opening the passenger door for him. Sarah took one more glance at the entrance while she was strapping herself into her seatbelt. Pat was still waiting.

The Lotus pulled away from the kerb outside the school

with a noise and abruptness that made heads turn. For all her intellect and sophistication, Sarah Challen was a rich man's daughter, and she was not accustomed to thwarted desire.

When Brack emerged from the school building, Pat took a step forward, then hesitated. Her husband had quickly been collared by the ITN reporter she had seen on television a few nights ago and was obviously being set up for an interview.

She had turned away when she heard Paul's voice calling her.

'Excuse me for a moment,' he apologized to Nick Rowe when he saw she had stopped.

'Pat, you came!' he said, striding towards her, beaming with pleasure.

'I'm glad I did.'

Brack looked embarrassed. 'I'd like to take you out to lunch –'

Pat smiled and filled in the rest for him. 'But you're too busy.' They stood looking at each other, almost shyly, for a couple of moments. 'You're doing well, Paul,' she said softly. 'Never mind about lunch. Just promise me you won't overdo it!'

Brack shrugged. 'Do I ever?'

'See you later,' she said, with a nod in the direction of the waiting TV crew.

Brack took her arm. 'Will you stay until the end of the day?'

'That's what I came for. Hardly be worth the trip otherwise.'

'Then I will see you later.'

Harold Harlan sprawled sound asleep in his well-padded armchair, lost in a dreamless unconsciousness such as only double jet-lag can produce. The television set in front of him played on.

'From Heathbridge, Nick Rowe reports . . .'

Sophie Ferris got quietly up from her chair and poured a

scotch into a tumbler on the drinks cabinet. Thus armed, she dared approach the slumbering Harlan.

Nick Rowe was beginning his report: 'The inquiry was scheduled to open with a brief statement about procedure from the inspector,' he said to camera. 'But Justice Wilkinson was challenged almost immediately by the man who has emerged as chief spokesman for the objectors, Dr Paul Brack . . .'

'It's Paul, Harold,' Sophie said, giving Harlan a gentle nudge. He opened his eyes, jolted upright and fought to focus on the screen. 'And I thought you might need this,' she added, handing him the whisky.

Harlan stared morosely at the screen as Rowe outlined the course of Brack's duel with the inspector. He had a feeling this was going to be a bad night.

Pat Brack arrived home in time to catch the end of Rowe's introduction. Oliver and Angela were littered around the room when she came in, and her son was the first to acknowledge her presence.

'Hello, Mum,' he said. 'Was it as much fun as it sounds?'

Pat smiled enigmatically. 'In what respect?'

At Sarah's flat, she and Brian Fletcher sat watching, too. The interview with Brack was beginning.

'I hope also that the widest possible audience will see that the AGR is the worst of some terrible nuclear options open to us; that the American Pressurized Water Reactor is in other ways just as bad; that the next stage in the pipeline of fission development, the Fast Breeder Reactor, is even more hazardous to the health and safety of this planet; and that . . .'

Fletcher suddenly launched himself at the television and clicked it off.

'Don't ask me, will you?' Sarah said angrily.

'I'm going to have to listen to that man for the next God knows how many weeks,' Fletcher told her.

Sarah got up deliberately, walked over and switched on the set again, leaving him to make his exit, glancing venomously as he went.

'I haven't rejected counsel,' Brack was saying now. 'But I only decided it was necessary to do this job forty-eight hours ago, and there hasn't been time to brief anyone.' Then he smiled, boyishly and with a touch of arrogance. 'But I am beginning to enjoy it.'

Sarah couldn't help smiling back.

Harlan, however, was finding it hard to smile.

'My purpose,' Brack was telling him from the screen. 'Is to argue the nuclear toss, not to provide the setting for some quaintly choreographed legal charade. I don't give a fig for the niceties of legal etiquette, provided the facts get a fair hearing.'

Then the camera took the viewers back to a brief parting shot of Rowe signing off in the school playground, with the words: 'So this inquiry has already been stamped with the personality of Dr Brack, and the battle between him and the inspector, Justice Wilkinson, will resume tomorrow.'

'He's certainly getting the coverage,' Sophie said tentatively.

'All right!' Harlan's savage rebuke brought a silence in which they both heard the newsreader's voice:

'And after a lively debate on nuclear policy in the House of Commons tonight, the government had a comfortable majority of fifty-two.'

Harlan pressed the set's remote control switch with one hand and downed the remains of his large scotch with the other. The newsreader, bearer of bad news, vanished in an explosive blip.

'Dammit,' Harlan muttered. 'And damn Paul Brack.'

Predictably, the one interested party who was not watching the Nick Rowe report was Paul Brack. He sat at the battered desk that had been set aside for him in a spare classroom at the Heathbridge school and checked yet again through his notes on Swedish advances in fluidized bed combustion techniques – methods that, he knew from his own work with Harlan, required only two-fifths of the coal used in a normal power station to produce the same amount of energy, and cost about two-thirds as much to build. He needed backups for fusion, his own professional pet field. And he needed an unanswerable core to his argument – the positive side of the equation he had to put over to the inquiry and, more importantly, to the public. If anyone would still be listening weeks from now. . . . Of course, today had been satisfactory. There had been the confrontation with Wilkinson, the TV interview, and there would be some good press pieces tomorrow, but the inquiry wasn't a one-day event: it would drag on, rightly, until he had managed to get the alternatives to nuclear power discussed as they had never been discussed before. The test would be whether the press would still be interested then, when the arguments were not about personalities but about what seemed like abstruse technical details, the kind that bored their readers. Well, Brack thought drily, someone would have to make sure they sat up and took notice, whatever. . . .

He was almost dropping with weariness, but he worked on, picking more papers from the two old suitcases that acted as his portable filing system. They had let him use the kitchens earlier to make coffee, but now those were locked up, as was every room except the bare classroom that was his makeshift office.

The door opened. Brack turned to see a security man standing in the entrance, shuffling from foot to foot with embarrassment.

'Ah . . . it's gone ten o'clock, sir,' the man said.

Brack shrugged. 'Look,' he suggested, 'why don't you just leave me the key and I'll lock up when I go.'

'You're joking, of course, sir?' The security man laughed nervously. 'I mean, there's half the atom secrets in the country sitting around in this place.'

Brack gazed at him for a moment, then chuckled. The man looked confused and offended.

'And the other half's in here,' Brack explained, throwing open the second of his suitcases – which was empty.

The security man edged over to inspect the case, then realized his leg was being pulled. He shuffled back towards the door, reddening. Very funny. Talk about mad bloody scientists. . . .

8

The inquiry went on – once Justice Wilkinson had granted Brack and the objectors their fourth assessor. That victory caused a small eruption in the media, keeping up interest, but as the proceedings continued into their second, then their third week, the cameras disappeared, local stringers took over press coverage, and attendances in the public seats thinned out. The course of the Heathbridge Inquiry was following a painfully predictable pattern; the kind of pattern that benefited the applicants, who when it came to the dull, soul-destroying slog of detail on detail could out-pound the amateurs.

George Spiking had gone back to his union fiefdom, leaving Barbara Richards as TUCANE's representative, at this stage little more than an observer. On the applicants' side, Brian Fletcher had taken over the day-to-day work. And Pat Brack kept coming, though most of the time she wasn't at all sure why.

Brack was on his feet this Friday afternoon, facing a relaxed, quietly probing Brian Fletcher across the stretch of floor between the objectors' and applicants' tables. The aggressive side of the UKAEA's strategy, as agreed between Fletcher and Phillips before the inquiry, was taking shape. Fletcher's task was to undermine Brack's credentials while at the same time keeping the big stick of the Official Secrets Act discreetly but clearly visible, and he was currently in the process of hammering that one home yet again.

'Don't you think, Dr Brack,' Fletcher said slowly,

almost lazily, 'that it is irresponsible of you to use your status as an ex-nuclear scientist' – he emphasized the 'ex-' with subtle care – 'to hint at heinous activities and attitudes within the organization that you chose to leave in order to join a private, commercial undertaking?' He paused and smiled coldly. 'After all, there are matters of which the general public are necessarily kept – shall we say – aware only in broad outline. It seems to me a cheap and easy way of whipping that lack of precise knowledge into hysteria for your own political and commercial purposes, to hint at dangerous practices of which you can have no very recent experience. . . .'

Brack shook his head and smiled. 'Recent enough,' he said pugnaciously. 'And there are a number of scientists within the Authority who share my concern and with whom I remain in contact. Morale is extremely low amongst sections of our so-called nuclear élite, as you must yourself be aware –'

'That's simply not true!' Fletcher sprang to his feet, casting aggrieved glances at the inspector. 'I don't accept any such thing. It's an outrageous slur!'

Justice Wilkinson sighed. 'Do you have any evidence to justify that remark, Dr Brack?'

'Oh, yes,' Brack said. 'But by your own ruling, sir, it is unfortunately inadmissible.'

Brack threw up his hands and turned in mock despair to the public seats.

The inspector and Fletcher exchanged wary looks. Their chief tormentor had already been warned about the Official Secrets Act.

'So perhaps we could return to the question we were originally . . . at least endeavouring to discuss?'

Fletcher, back in his seat, took a moment to reply. When he did, he spoke carefully, as if from a rehearsed text.

'I should have thought that the reason for secrecy over a matter like laser enrichment of uranium was perfectly obvious to any sensible mind,' he said.

Brack nodded encouragingly and made a beckoning

motion, making it clear that he was entitled to more of an explanation than that. Meanwhile, a man in the public seats, who had hitherto been engrossed in his tabloid newspaper, suddenly put his paper down and pricked up his ears. He whispered something to the uniformed policeman sitting next to him and began to take notes. The gentleman from the Special Branch had been aroused.

If Brack had failed to notice the policeman's interest, Fletcher certainly did. He stared hard in their direction when he resumed his recitation.

'We live in a dangerous society,' he intoned. 'One which twice already in this century has exhibited a willingness to indulge in world-wide military destruction. Military technology has provided for a degree of stability between the major powers which is less than perfect but certainly better than the first forty-five years of this century could have led us to expect. The greatest threat to that stability is now posed by the inadequacy of the world's energy resources to cope with its growing needs. Again it is nuclear technology which offers us the most promising means of reducing that threat.'

Fletcher saw the look of contempt in Brack's expression and looked away, keying himself up for the knock-out punch.

'But,' he went on. 'As Dr Brack himself proclaims in his book, energy is power – not only motive power but also actual political power. Therefore society must take the strongest possible measures to prevent that power from falling into the wrong hands. One of the most obvious steps in that direction is to limit opportunities of access to the details of nuclear technology by individual groups, or foreign powers who might have reason to abuse it. For that reason, sir,' Fletcher finished firmly, addressing the inspector, 'it would be quite improper for me to continue to answer Dr Brack's present line of questioning.'

He sat back and studied his papers, apparently confident that he had made an end to the matter.

Justice Wilkinson nodded, then turned to Brack. 'Do you accept that, Dr Brack?'

'No,' said Brack in a loud, clear voice, gazing at Fletcher as if he were some unclean animal that had wandered into a civilized room.

'Then I rule on it,' the inspector said sharply. 'Further discussion of this issue must cease. Have you any other questions for Dr Fletcher?'

'Yes,' Brack confirmed, rising from his seat once more. He turned to Fletcher. 'I would like to know,' he said, 'whether he can show that security measures taken to prevent the dissemination of classified information have been completely successful.'

His manner seemed serious, but there were telltale signs of mockery at the corners of his mouth.

'Of course not,' Fletcher said quickly. 'That would be tantamount to revealing the very information the measures were designed to protect.'

Brack smiled knowingly. He was back on the offensive again, and clearly enjoying it. Fletcher looked to the inspector for aid, and Wilkinson responded.

'Dr Brack, I hope that this is not a continuation of the same line of questioning as I have ruled inadmissible?' he asked.

'No, sir. This is something else entirely.'

Fletcher, meanwhile, had been using the respite for some urgent whispering with the UKAEA's legal adviser to his right at the applicants' table. He was beginning to show the strain, Brack noted with satisfaction, and pressed on quickly.

'There are actually some rather spectacular examples of how those measures have failed, are there not?' he declared, aiming his remarks into the half-empty hall, as if addressing a group of students. 'It was not possible to prevent so-called "atom secrets" from falling into the hands of the Russians. Nor was it possible to prevent a shipload of plutonium from falling into the hands of the Israelis, thus enabling a small nation at the centre of one of the world's trouble spots to join the nuclear club. Nor even to prevent Pakistan from turning a low-level civil nuclear operation into weapons-building capability . . .'

The inspector intervened. 'The fact that the most elaborate systems can sometimes fail, Dr Brack, does not invalidate –'

Brack threw up his arms in delight at such manna from heaven. 'Exactly, sir!' he exclaimed. 'You could not have made my point more succinctly!'

For the first time in these three weeks, despite previous provocations, Justice Wilkinson came close to publicly losing his temper. It was a spectacular sight: his smooth, almost epicene features reddened; the veins in his forehead became prominent; he rapped the table in front of him with his bare knuckles.

'I will not be interrupted, Dr Brack!'

'No, sir. I merely wanted to point out, in passing, that you had nicely reinforced my point for me. . . .'

Then he laughed, and for a moment it seemed as if Justice Wilkinson might crown a distinguished and blameless career on the Bench with an apoplectic seizure.

'I order you to be silent!' he bellowed, then, with an effort, caught himself and took refuge in mopping his forehead with a tissue from the box on his table. The inspector coughed, looked at the ceiling, fighting to recover his dignity. 'I must also remind you again,' he said after some time, more calmly now, 'I laid down a condition at the beginning of this hearing that no evidence whatsoever that could be prejudicial to national security would be admissible. That condition stands.'

The Special Branch man and his companion were sitting upright with their attention riveted on the dispute, their faces relaxed but alert, oddly like linesmen at a tennis match waiting for the ball to kick up some chalk and be ruled out.

Brack, however, was also flushed with anger.

'And may I, too, remind the tribunal that this is the third salient point that I have been prevented from making because the witness has been allowed to scuttle away under the skirts of official secrecy!' he barked.

There was an embarrassed silence in the hall, followed by murmurings from the public seats and one or two brave shouts of: 'Shame!' On the dais, Sir Frank Sutton began to sort his papers and stack them with ostentatious deliberation. The Special Branch man unfolded his arms and jotted something down in his ring notebook. Justice Wilkinson and Brack stared furiously at each other for a long moment like daredevil schoolboys, Fletcher completely forgotten, before the inspector regained sufficient of his *sang-froid* to take Sutton's hint.

'I think it's been a long, hard week,' he announced, with a fair attempt at Olympian detachment. 'I think we would all benefit from a cooling-off period. Accordingly, the hearing is adjourned until ten a.m. on Monday.'

Mrs Minchin stood just inside the door of Brack's classroom 'office', slightly nervous and reluctant to make a social *faux pas*, for she knew that Brack and his wife were estranged.

'If you're going to stay in Heathbridge over the weekend,' she said. 'I wonder if you would . . . both . . . care to join my husband and myself for lunch on Sunday?'

Brack was seated at his desk, with Pat opposite him by the blackboard on an adult-sized arm chair that had been purloined from the staff room. Realizing Mrs Minchin's dilemma, she smiled easily and shook her head.

'I'd love to,' she said. 'Thanks for your kind invitation, but unfortunately I have to get back to children. But Paul . . .?'

Brack looked at her, realized there was no reproach in her mention of the children this time, and nodded. 'Yes . . . yes . . . thanks, Margaret. That would be very pleasant.'

'Good,' the mayor said with evident relief. 'Come about mid-day for a glass of sherry.'

'Fine. See you then.'

Mrs Minchin paused at the door, as if feeling she had to

say something to Pat. 'I think he stands a chance of winning this for us, Mrs Brack,' she told her. 'We're all very grateful. . . .'

Then she said her farewells and disappeared along the corridor, an upright, solid figure in tweed, twinset and brogues.

Brack grinned at Pat, and she smiled back in unspoken, shared gratitude for the chance to be alone.

'Marvellous lady,' he chuckled. 'Say what you like, but the Mrs Minchins of this world are the backbone of our lives. And get her kind going on the nuclear issue . . .'

Pat, however, was thoughtful. She nodded absently, then stood up and sat on his desk, looking directly at him.

'Paul,' she began slowly. 'I think Brian Fletcher's setting a trap for you.'

Brack shrugged matter-of-factly. 'Yes,' he said. 'Which leads me to my first question: what are you like on national security law?'

'Not my field at all,' Pat answered, frowning. 'I should be very careful. The times are not auspicious for civil liberty.'

'When are they ever?'

'I told you,' Pat said with a strained smile. 'Certainly not now. Look, Paul, we have ten per cent of the population out of work; racial tensions are running high; we're on the crest of a juvenile crime wave. And on the international scene, statesmanship has given way to old-fashioned sabre-rattling. It's a time when the liberal mice who occasionally roar in our society will be keeping their mouths firmly shut. . . .'

Brack was looking at her with a new interest. He nodded and gestured for her to go on.

'All I can say,' she continued, 'is that if you're thinking of taking on the state, Paul, you shouldn't count on much in the way of support from the weaker brethren. And I think you should take some highly qualified advice.'

'I'm asking for it, now,' Brack said, standing up and taking her hands in his.

'Oh, I'm neither qualified nor without prejudice . . .' Pat murmured awkwardly.

'But you are my wife. . . .'

They embraced warmly, like affectionate friends making up for a misunderstanding. A long misunderstanding. There was a knock on the door and Barbara Richardson walked in with a folder under her arm, catching Brack and Pat still in each other's arms beside the desk.

'Oh, I'm sorry . . .' Barbara said, coming to a halt inside the door, cut off from retreat but unwilling to come in any further.

Pat withdrew from her husband's embrace, patting her hair. 'It's all right,' she said with a helpless smile. 'I'm just leaving.'

Sarah Challen came into the living room of the flat and put down the tray with the coffee percolator, cups and milk jug. Brian had been brooding during the trip back from Weymouth, and had been uncharacteristically silent during dinner. He was clearly building up to some kind of revelation, she had thought, though she was in no mood to prod him into pouring out his troubles to her. In fact, she wasn't at all sure what the hell she did want from Fletcher any more.

In the event, Brian broke his silence during the coffee. Predictably.

'Andrei Sakharov,' he said suddenly. 'Andrei Sakharov says it's in the Soviet Union's interest to exploit and create energy shortages in the West. Whether or not Paul Brack is consciously working for the enemy, I don't know. . . .'

Here we go again, Sarah thought bitterly. Round ninety-three. 'Do you mean what I think you mean?' she said sardonically. 'My God, you do! And we used to make jokes about *his* paranoia!'

Brian, however, showed not a flicker of humour or even irony. 'You noticed who he sat next to at the beginning of the inquiry?' he continued stolidly. Sarah made no answer.

but he nodded grimly all the same; this was a monologue addressed to himself. 'Of course, Spiking's gone home now. Didn't take Comrade George long to realize the cause was in capable hands. . . .'

'For God's sake, Brian,' Sarah interrupted, 'it seems to me that all Paul wants is a little more freedom of information, and he's not alone in that.' She would try to be reasonable, she told herself. This absurdity had to be argued against, if only for . . . for Paul's sake. 'Paul's always had a phobia about secrecy,' she continued. 'He never saw how it could be consistent with a scientist's search for truth. We used to admire him for that. At least I did.'

Fletcher laughed derisively and flopped back in his armchair. It was not a pretty sound, or an attractive sight. 'You were always politically naïve,' he said. 'Don't you understand the nature of the challenge he's making?'

Condescension was too much, coming from a mindless apparatchik like this. Christ, she should have paid more attention to her father. He had never said he disapproved of Brian, but he had thrown out enough hints.

'I understand that you've begun to talk like an unconscionable bigot!' she shot back furiously.

It was like water off a duck's back. 'Thanks,' Brian muttered. 'But don't be sentimental about friend Brack, Sarah. He's lost his nerve and his sense of direction. And he's frightened of middle age, terrified of losing his position as a front runner. A rat denouncing the race –'

'Make up your mind. Just a minute ago he was being directed by Moscow!'

Then there was a snort from Brian, followed by a smouldering silence. Sarah gulped down the rest of her coffee and collected their cups, rather more noisily than was strictly necessary. As she made her way to the kitchen with the tray, she heard Brian yawn.

'God, I feel exhausted,' he said at her retreating back.

If it was meant to be a sly excuse. Sarah had no intention of letting him get away with it. She turned on her heel, eyes icy with contempt, and fired her well-aimed barb.

'Exhausted?' she hissed. 'What with? The strain of licking dear old Norman's arse?'

She had slammed the kitchen door firmly behind her before Fletcher had a chance to reply.

Harlan, in shirt sleeves and with a whisky glass in one hand, nodded as he spoke into the phone.

'All right, Pat,' he said soothingly. 'Thanks for letting me know. And I'll come up with something, don't worry. 'Bye . . .'

He put the receiver down and stared at it balefully. 'Though God knows why a level-headed woman like you ever married the fool,' he murmured.

Sophie, curled up on the sofa listening to the conversation, raised an enquiring eyebrow.

'What's the problem?' she asked lightly.

Harlan sighed. 'Pat fears,' he said with mock deliberation, 'that "they" are deliberately goading Paul into being indiscreet.' Sophie laughed, but Harlan shook his head thoughtfully. 'Yes, ha ha. But I don't like the sound of it. Call it a hunch . . .'

'Would you like me to have a word with Alan Stevenson?'

Harlan pondered, then nodded. Stevenson was the smoothest and most expensive civil-liberties solicitor in town. The priciest insurance, but the best. 'Yes . . . yes . . . That's not a bad idea. See if he'd be willing to drive down to Weymouth with me on Monday, will you?'

Sophie took over the phone. Harlan walked over to the panoramic window of his flat and stared out over the brilliantly lit London skyline. He wearily put his hands to his face, then dropped them and spoke softly to the world out there:

'Paul Brack,' he said. 'I do believe that if I were Henry II, king of England, I would say you were behaving like a troublesome priest.'

*

Brack left his hotel very early on the Monday morning, and arrived at the inquiry hall in Heathbridge in time to see the caretaker open up the building. By the time the other participants began to drift in, he was seated at his usual place, on the table to the left of inspector's dais, watching with keen interest as the new arrivals took their seats. On each chair in the hall, and at each place on the tables, he had laid a xeroxed copy of a small, slim pamphlet that he had typed himself over the weekend.

The Special Branch man and his uniformed companion arrived, picked up the copies on their chairs, glanced at them briefly, then buried themselves in their newspapers. Mrs Minchin settled at the table next to Brack and leafed through the pamphlet with a puzzled expression, clearly at a loss as to its significance. The first to show any real reaction was Barbara Richards, who drew a deep breath when she read the first page and then carried on reading, her jaw set in a tense line.

Brian Fletcher arrived hurriedly, slightly later than usual, and almost missed the pamphlet, so busy was he getting out the contents of his well-filled briefcase. When it did catch his attention, however, his period of study was no longer than thirty seconds. He stood up, shot a glance filled with purest venom at Brack, then walked quickly over to where the Special Branch man was still checking up on Spurs' performance on the previous Saturday. After a short, whispered conversation, the plain clothes man picked up his copy of the pamphlet and accompanied Fletcher out into the vestibule of the hall, leaving the uniformed man to keep an unwavering eye on Brack.

Fletcher and the Special Branch man moved aside at the exit to allow two other men to come into the hall: Harlan and Alan Stevenson were in a hurry; the majesty of the law was not.

'Good morning, Harold,' Brack said mildly when he saw Harlan and the lawyer advancing down the aisle towards him.

Harlan waved a hand to identify Stevenson. 'Paul, take it easy, I've brought a solicitor to sort this out . . .' he said, quickening his step.

Brack was too agile for him. He stepped sideways and sprang up onto the dais. From there he could see that Pat was also coming into the hall, but her appearance had no apparent effect. Brack summoned everyone's attention by banging hard on the inspector's table with Justice Wilkinson's official gavel.

'Good morning, ladies and gentlemen,' he announced in a firm clear voice. 'I want to explain this.'

Brack held up a copy of the pamphlet.

'The pamphlet you will each have found on your chairs is a brief summary of the state of research into the enrichment of uranium by laser. It is classified information under the laws of this country, for the publication of which I expect to be arrested in a few minutes' time.'

Pat, meanwhile, had reached the front of the hall and was standing with Harlan and Stevenson, helpless, all colour drained from her face.

'Paul, no!' she shouted.

Stevenson gestured in the direction of the copies on the chairs. 'I'm afraid it's probably too late, Mrs Brack,' he said. 'The material has, technically speaking, been published.'

Brack continued stubbornly, avoiding looking at the stricken figure of his wife.

'When the technology outlined here is perfected – and for all I know it may already be in widespread secret use – it will mean that literally thousands of laboratories, government or private, throughout the world will be able to enrich uranium for the purpose of making nuclear bombs.'

The audience gazed at him in shocked silence. Pat hid her face in her hands. Harlan stood helplessly, hands on hips, staring down at the polished floor and shaking his head. Brack snatched a glance at the back of the hall, saw he was still safe for the moment, and continued.

'I came here at the request of the objectors as an expert,'

he said. 'But at several crucial junctures I have been prevented from bringing my expert knowledge to bear on the issues by the invoking of the Official Secrets Act. As a consequence it has become plain to me that the official secrecy behind which the United Kingdom Atomic Energy Authority operates has the effect not so much of protecting our national security as of concealing the truth about nuclear lunacy.'

The door at the back of the hall opened a chink, then closed abruptly. Brack pressed on, knowing he was now running out of time.

'Our world stands much closer to the brink of self-destruction than most of us are allowed to believe,' he said quickly. 'We are protected from a terrifying reality by the Official Secrets Act. Unless, however, we face that reality, there will be no national, nor indeed any other kind of human interest left to protect. I have published this pamphlet not because I *want* bombs to be mass produced by anyone, from small nations to terrorist groups – in fact, I don't think my act will make the slightest difference to that possibility. No, my aim is to further public awareness and knowledge. You, ladies and gentlemen, are all witnesses to this act of criminal treason – and I hope that many of you will support me in this deliberate challenge to a diabolically restrictive and dangerous law. Thank you.'

He relaxed for a moment and smiled, as if a huge burden had been removed from him, then straightened his back and stepped down towards the Special Branch man and the policeman, who were approaching from the front of the aisle.

'Now,' he asked calmly. 'How would you like this bit to happen?'

9

Brack watched in numbed silence while the Special Branch sergeant sorted through the objects they had found in his pockets. There was something unsettling about the thorough, precise way he muttered instructions to the uniformed PC who was cataloguing the stuff. It must be deliberate, of course; part of the ritual humiliation of the accused, the beginning of the softening-up process. The Hindus might say: 'You are what you eat', but the same went for what you carried around in your pockets. To have two strangers sifting through your possessions was a new, intimidating experience.

'One wallet, notes to the value of twenty-three pounds,' the sergeant recited in a bored voice. 'Driving licence . . . no licence, Dr Brack?' he asked, looking up from the table.

Brack met the question with a tight smile. 'My vehicle, not being lethal, does not require a licence,' he said archly.

The sergeant looked at him blankly, then continued: 'Postage stamps to the value of eighty-four pence . . .'

He had been brought to the interview room at Heathbridge police station straight from the inquiry hall. Strange, Brack thought, but one passed police stations every day, tucked away in ordinary streets, and hitherto they had always seemed a normal, even comforting part of the urban scene, blue lamp and red brick, functional citadels of order. Until the day came when you entered one, not as a free citizen but as a prisoner. Then they swallowed you up, and you realized that was what they were designed to do.

The uniformed PC had finished noting the objects down

in his little cloth-bound book. He turned it round and pushed it gently across the table towards Brack, along with a biro.

'Sign there, please, Dr Brack,' he said with punctilious politeness. 'To show that you agree this to be an accurate record.'

Brack glanced quickly down the list and signed. 'Am I now to be charged?' he asked the sergeant, pushing the book back towards the PC.

The Special Branch man shook his head slowly. He was in his late twenties, thickly built and square-faced. His terse correctness so far hid a pushy, aggressive side, Brack suspected. He looked as though he could turn very nasty if given the opportunity.

'We have reason to suspect that an offence has been committed,' the sergeant said. 'You are being detained to help us with inquiries, Dr Brack.'

Brack almost smiled at the hackneyed euphemism, but something in the Special Branch man's cold, curiously empty eyes warned him not to mess around. But he met the man's gaze; that was part of the game. 'When can I see a solicitor?' he said.

'Whenever an interview can be arranged that would not interfere with our inquiries,' the sergeant said. The words rolled off his tongue as if they had been learned by heart. He stood up, straightening his tie, and added with a hint of relish: 'At the moment, though, it would.'

The Special Branch man strode over to the door and opened it.

'Okay,' he said crisply to someone outside in the corridor. 'You can take him down now.'

Another uniformed PC appeared. Brack got to his feet expectantly, still keeping a level eye on the sergeant but inwardly dazed by the curt efficiency of the whole process. So this was it, after all the talking and the thinking. Suddenly he could think of nothing more to say. He walked out between the two PCs, each maintaining a gentle pressure on his arm.

Sergeant Callaway of the Special Branch watched as the door closed behind his prisoner. When Brack was safely out of his sight, he took off his jacket, sat down at the table and lit a cigarette. Then he began to comb methodically through Brack's diary, noting down names and addresses. They'd teach the cocky bastard. By the time his superior got in touch, Callaway intended to have the show well on the road.

Pat Brack felt her hopes rise momentarily when she saw the duty sergeant on the desk at Heathbridge police station. In contrast with the hard-faced Special Branch man, this sergeant was a big, jolly looking character, straight out of the kind of TV police series they used to run before 'The Sweeny' came along and made cops just as foul-mouthed and violent as the criminals they were confronting.

Stevenson went straight to the desk and showed his card.

'My name is Stevenson,' he announced smoothly. 'Solicitor, of Ridley, Stevenson and Company. Dr Brack is my client. I am asking for my right of access to him.'

'Ah yes,' the officer said. 'Dr Brack is presently helping us with inquiries, sir . . .'

The pleasant Dorset burr and the deferential manner were still there, but Pat sensed a subtle stiffening in the man's attitude.

'How long are the preliminaries likely to take?' Stevenson asked.

The sergeant sucked in his cheeks. 'Oh, I can't say, sir. . . . Perhaps you might telephone at about lunchtime?'

Stevenson turned to Pat and Harlan with a wry smile, then back to the desk officer. 'I would prefer to speak to someone in authority, if I might,' he said.

Pat, taking the cue, sat down wearily on a bench opposite the desk. She could see this would take some time.

Harlan did not join her. He whispered something to Stevenson, then headed towards the door. He had to make a phone call, he said purposefully.

Pat nodded indifferently. Life had to go on, she supposed. Stevenson was still pressing the duty sergeant for an interview with his superior. The game of saving Paul Brack from himself was beginning to enter its end phase.

At St Andrew's Church Hall, the objectors were in session to consider their position, leaving the inquiry to continue without them. Mrs Minchin, in the chair, had been unwise enough to warn against over-reaction to Brack's arrest.

'That's the trouble with us bloody English!' Barbara Richards exclaimed. 'As soon as anyone shows any real balls in dealing with the establishment, we start apologizing for it. "Over-reaction", my ass!'

Mrs Minchin winced visibly. 'Perhaps it was unfortunate choice of words, Barbara,' she said with a prim smile. 'I think we're all agreed, though, that we are getting considerably more than we bargained for with Dr Brack?'

'Because he saw what the real issue was, while we were all fiddling around with peripherals. *He* showed *us* what we should really be objecting to!'

That brought a brief, thoughtful silence. Colin Tansley, representative of the Council for the Preservation of Rural England, leaned forward. 'The question is, however, where do we go from here?' he asked mildly.

Barbara Richards fixed the rest of them with an earnest stare. 'Well,' she said. 'Boycotting the inquiry's going to do no good at all. We might as well drop our objections altogether and let the CEGB go right ahead and do what they like.'

'Am I right to assume that you've got some specific suggestions to make, Barbara?' Tansley chipped in.

Barbara Richards nodded energetically. 'Yes, I have. First, I think we should demand that the inquiry be adjourned, at least until Brack is either released or charged. If he is charged, then I think we should claim that since major issues in our case will then be *sub judice* the inquiry will be unable to complete its hearings until they have been resolved in the courts.' She gazed intently round the table.

'Third, I think we should organize a Brack Defence Committee. After all,' she emphasized heavily, 'the man was arrested while engaged in active service on our behalf. Fourth, I think we should contact George Spiking immediately and invite him to resume the job of co-ordinating and leading our case.'

Mrs Minchin looked uncomfortable, but she nodded agreement with the TUCANE representative's proposals. 'All right,' she said. 'Does anyone else have any suggestions? Or should we take Barbara's programme as the basis for an agenda and debate it point by point?'

Barbara Richards sighed in exasperation as the man from Friends of the Earth, Roger Barnes, raised his hand to speak.

'By all means debate it, friends,' she said acidly. 'But just remember that while we're sitting here discussing agendas, the inquiry's hard at work producing whitewash. . . .'

The objectors' seats were empty at the Inquiry Hall. Brian Fletcher, quite unfazed by the absence of his opponents as a result of the day's bizarre start, was able to make his statement without fear of specialist cross-questioning. There were one or two hecklers at the back, but he could handle them.

'We ought, I think, to consider ourselves a mature society,' he intoned. 'This very inquiry is a highly sophisticated social mechanism for assessing the arguments for and against a major technological development. And I welcome it. I believe we should have confidence in our institutions and their ability to exploit and control the wealth of individual scientific talent in our society and to harness it to our common pursuit of progress, with the aim of creating a better life on this planet.' He paused and smiled at his audience. 'When it became possible for man to fly,' Fletcher continued, like a teacher addressing a group of willing but none-too-bright children, 'our ancestors had the vision to appreciate the enormous benefits that aviation could bring. So, far from banning it, they contrived a complex framework of rules which we all agree to observe in the interests of general safety. . . .'

'Aircraft still crash!' someone bellowed from the back of the hall.

Fletcher nodded politely. 'Indeed, sir,' he agreed. 'But no one would argue, I think, that the suffering caused by an occasional accident outweighs the benefits we have all derived from air travel.'

'Yes, they would!'

This time Fletcher ignored the interruption. It was all clumsy, parish-pump stuff, in any case. Nothing he couldn't handle.

'It's all a question of balance, of risk equated against benefit,' he said. 'And we are here presenting the case for the expansion of an energy programme based on nuclear fission in the reasoned belief that its benefits . . .'

'For the people in London!' the heckler shouted, still game, and brought a stern rebuke from the inspector.

'. . . that its benefits,' Fletcher concluded easily, 'in relation to other means of energy production, are high; and that its risks, in comparison with other sources, are low.'

He sat down. They were due for the lunch adjournment in a few minutes. Without Paul Brack, this was going to be easy.

Pat Brack sat on her son's bed while Oliver described his visit from the Special Branch. The boy looked pale, but the cause was anger rather than terror, she noted with relief and perverse pride.

Oliver jabbed a thumb at the 'Protest and Survive' poster on his bedroom wall. '"Following in Daddy's footsteps, are we, sonny?" the man said. Christ, Mum, he was revolting,' he said.

Pat smiled, stood up and walked to the stairs, her arm round her son's shoulder. 'What other questions did they ask?' she probed as they made their way down.

Oliver tensed. 'It was all personal stuff. I didn't know whether to answer or not.'

‘What kind of things?’

‘Oh, how long have you and Dad been living apart? Are you officially separated? How often does Dad come and visit? Does he use his study when he comes?’

Pat saw his nose wrinkle with distaste at the memory. In the living room, Angela was waiting with a large gin for her mother. Pat sipped gratefully. God knows how she had managed the drive up from Dorset; it had felt like a bad dream. But still it was good to be home . . . where she should have been hours previously, by the sound of it.

‘Thanks, darling,’ she said to Angela. ‘I’m just sorry you had to put with everything without me. I stayed down there because . . . I just hoped I could get a message to him through the solicitor, but . . .’

She shook her head and sat down. Soon enough this numbness would wear off, it was one of the mind’s protective devices. Then she would be vulnerable.

Angela sat down on the sofa beside Pat and took her mother’s hand. They sat in silence while Pat fortified herself with her gin, then said: ‘Did . . . did they take anything away?’

‘They spent ages in the study, but I don’t think they took anything,’ Angela said.

Pat laughed nervously. ‘Nobody can find anything in there. Not even Paul,’ she said, desperately trying to lighten things.

Then she caught Oliver’s eye. The boy’s stare was merciless, even accusing.

‘Why did he do it, Mum?’ he said baldly.

‘Oh, Ollie, I don’t know!’ Pat answered, then leaned her head on Angela’s shoulder and gave way to the tears that had been threatening to come all day.

Chief Inspector Peter Seymour of the Special Branch enjoyed his job; it enabled him to meet interesting people and, indeed, gave him access to a great deal of information that the ordinary public knew nothing about. There were some who thought it odd that a man of his impeccably middle-class, even intellectual tastes and habits should volunteer for the life of a political policeman; the SB lacked the glamour of the 'James Bond' departments, for it usually handled the messy, trivial cases, and its operatives were really no more than jumped-up cops. Apart from anything else, however, Seymour liked to think that the SB needed men like himself, who believed in the rapier rather than the bludgeon. It helped to balance the presence of men like – to be honest – Sergeant Callaway. The young ex-CID man was tough and ambitious, a believer in conviction at any price, which was why Seymour had hurried to meet him in Oxford before they came over here to Brack's flat. So long as one kept an eye on Callaway, he was an asset. On that basis, they worked well together, the smooth and the rough, the old one-two. . . .

They had been searching the flat in Waldegrave for a little over twenty minutes. The rooms were in chaos, but that was not due to them: their training made them neat and unobtrusive when they went over a place. Seymour, seated at Brack's desk, snapped shut a file and sighed philosophically.

Callaway, who had been hunting round the piano in the corner of the room, even rummaging through the sheet music crammed into the hinged seat of the piano stool, was clearly feeling far from stoic. He straightened up and cursed roundly.

'So who thought it was necessary to come and "Tidy up", eh?' he growled.

Seymour shrugged. 'An interesting question,' he said. 'Here we have this man Brack, presenting the image of the knight in shining armour, tilting at the Official Secrets Act for the good of his and everyone else's soul. This,' he added, waving one hand at the mess, 'represents a rather different picture. Whoever's responsible was a professional. But why make such a mess if they knew what to look for and where to find it?'

'To divert us from the fact that they knew bloody well,' Callaway said.

'Ah,' Seymour suggested, with the palest ghost of a smile. 'The hand of Moscow?'

Callaway nodded stolidly. 'Something like that. Disguised to look as though it isn't.'

Seymour eased himself up from the chair and strolled round the flat, peeking into the bathroom, the bedroom. It was the same story: everything thrown about as if the place had been hit by a typhoon, and no sense or apparent system.

'Spies don't generally get up and announce their possession of classified information at public meetings – at least not in Dorset, they don't,' he said. 'If there was any link with the East, Brack's just broken it.'

'People do crazy things when they're under pressure,' Callaway suggested.

'But under pressure from whom? Or what? Oh, certainly these affairs can get very complicated. Brack's obviously not a straight agent for anyone. Which still leaves us with no idea of who did this little job here.'

Callaway picked up a magazine from the floor and began leafing through it, muttering: 'Buggered if I know, then.'

'Well, I think we're wasting our time here,' Seymour said. 'What goodies there ever were have been filched from under our noses.'

'Try his wife, then? She was out when I went to the house, still at Heathbridge. Or his boss?'

Seymour nodded. 'Every avenue will be followed, as the good book says,' he agreed. 'And I'm looking forward to meeting your Dr Brack. Tomorrow, I think, when he's had a little more time on his own to count his sins.'

When the two Special Branch officers got into their car and drove away from the flats, a neat, alert-looking man sitting opposite and a little down the street in a nondescript saloon followed their departure with punctilious attention. He had seen them leave empty-handed, which was useful to know. More importantly, he knew why, for in the boot of his own car sat a suitcase filled with documents, papers and effects from Paul Brack's flat.

The man started up the engine and the car moved away from the kerb. As he drove he began to whistle a Gilbert and Sullivan tune that had always been a favourite of his. The chorus line was: 'A policeman's lot is not a happy one . . .'

10

Harold Harlan sat at Brack's desk in Waldegrave House, leafing quickly through random selections of files. The office had been comprehensively tidied during the past couple of hours, but the contents of the suitcase removed from Brack's flat were spread around the desk top in considerable confusion. Harlan rubbed his eyes, then flung down the material he had been reading with a bellow of mingled anger and despair. He had driven up here from London at six a.m., after a sleepless night, and the strain was starting to tell.

'God!' he groaned. 'What the hell does Paul think he's been doing these past months? I don't know whether this stuff is actually classified, but the Special Branch would give their eye teeth to get hold of it, I can tell you that.'

John Foster, hovering at his elbow, nodded sympathetically. A soberly dressed ex-policeman in his late thirties, Foster was the best 'inquiry agent' in the business. Harlan had used him before when situations got a little fuzzy round the edges, and Foster was well paid to enter the grey areas of business secrecy, to check up on business associates – and enemies – when background was not readily available through the conventional channels. A telephone call from Heathbridge the previous morning, brief negotiations leading to agreement on a fat fee, and Foster had gone to Waldegrave to do the necessary.

Sophie Ferris, sitting across the table from Harlan, glanced at Foster, then handed her boss a sheet of typescript. There were still scraps of sellotape adhering to the corners where it had been torn from a flat surface, and one paragraph had been circled heavily in thick red felt pen.

'Perhaps this might provide some insights,' Sophie said.

'It was stuck to the wall in front of the typewriter at Dr Brack's flat, as if he wanted to be constantly reminded of it while he was working,' Foster explained.

Harlan grunted and proceeded to read out the encircled passage:

'Of course I believe it is both necessary and praiseworthy that people should defend themselves against the encroachment of nuclear power . . .' the paragraph began. 'If an injudiciously sited fission power station were to suffer a major accident, then twenty, thirty, perhaps even a hundred thousand people could be killed, and that is not a comfortable shadow in which to live an ordinary life. But of immeasurably greater significance to the future of this planet is the insane – and I use that word to the full value of its meaning – the insane proliferation of all kinds of nuclear weapons. It is against this madness that the efforts of ordinary people should now be directed in the interests of sheer survival . . .'

Harlan let the paper fall from his fingers and stared morosely at Sophie.

'Don't tell me,' he murmured. 'Max Challen, silver-haired doyen of the anti-nuclear movement, seducer of youth?'

'From a reprint of his speech to the Oxford Union last November,' Sophie confirmed. 'It provides some indication of why Paul went so overboard about the Heathbridge business.'

Harlan sighed. 'More than that,' he said, shaking his head in numbed disbelief. 'So Dr Brack's taken it upon himself to become a ban-the-bomber. . . .'

Foster coughed. 'The papers I . . . er . . . thought it wise to remove, Mr Harlan, seem mostly to have been assembled during the course of the last two or three months,' he said.

'And what about his house – I mean his wife's house in Oxford?' Harlan asked sharply.

Foster smiled in apology. 'I'm afraid Special Branch beat me there. I think they stopped off on their way up. Fortunate, really – gave me time to concentrate on the flat.'

'In any case, that may not be so catastrophic,' Sophie said. 'Paul cleared most of the stuff he needed to hand when he moved out last year. Apart from collecting and delivering the children, I get the impression Paul hasn't been home since Christmas.'

'Pat was at Heathbridge, though, don't forget,' Harlan said, drumming his fingers on the desk top thoughtfully. 'And the poor woman was far from unemotional in her involvement. I don't know how much she knew, but Pat looked like a person being torn apart. So the good doctor drags us all down with him.'

Suddenly he turned away from the other two, his eyes blazing with anger.

'For Christ's sake,' Harlan snarled. 'Why can't the man grow up? I'm damned if I've got time and money to spare changing his nappies for him –'

The telephone on the desk rang. Sophie picked it up quickly.

'Dr Brack's telephone. Yes. Right. I'll be down straight away.'

She replaced the phone and gazed helplessly at Harlan.

'Special Branch in reception,' she told him. 'It had to come. They want to look around in here, of course.'

Harlan got to his feet, anger and self-pity giving way to firm decision.

'All right, Foster. You clean up as much as you can in here before the gents from the Branch get this far. Put the material from the flat in the basement or somewhere,' he ordered the inquiry agent, then turned to Sophie Ferris. 'Sophie, you keep them entertained for as long as you possibly can. Tell them Brack's life-story – censored version, naturally. I'll be in my office, composing a few plausible answers. If – and only if – they want to see me, make sure someone rings me to give advance warning. Okay?'

He strode towards the door, then turned.

'You know, I should have stayed in the oil business,' he said with bitter humour. 'People were nice and simple. Corrupt, greedy, ruthless – and they only broke the law when it paid and when they knew they'd get away with it. God save me from the high-minded idiots I'm forced to employ in this game!'

Sergeant Callaway carefully jotted yet more down in his ring-notebook, and looked hard at Pat Brack.

'So,' he said. 'We have established that your husband was unhappy with some aspects of his work while you were in the United States. Tell me, was he a member of any anti-war organization or group in particular?'

'Oh no,' Pat answered hastily, unsettled by the line of his questioning. This relentless, hard-looking young policeman was worlds away from road safety posters and Dixon of Dock Green. He was the one who had talked to Oliver, and now she could understand her son's repugnance only too well. 'In that sense,' she continued, prodded by Callaway's insatiably searching gaze, 'Paul's a hopelessly unpolitical animal. He won't join any party or organization of any kind if he can help it, not even professional bodies. I suppose you could call him a maverick, a natural loner. . . .'

Callaway stopped writing in his notebook for a moment and looked interested. 'Sometimes such a step can't be helped, Mrs Brack,' he said mysteriously.

'What . . . what do you mean?'

'Well, we're sometimes a little indiscreet, aren't we?' Callaway explained with a cynical smile. 'We say things that would be better left unsaid. We do things we shouldn't. People get to know, and the price of their silence can be high. Like, maybe, getting involved with political organizations we'd prefer not to be involved with . . .'

Pat frowned, incredulous. 'Are you suggesting – no, you

can't be! – that Paul may have been forced into working on behalf of the Communists?'

'Wouldn't be the first time,' Callaway said. Then he shrugged, and his voice lost its edge of aggression. 'Of course,' he added, suddenly all sweet reason, 'I'm just trying to suggest new lines of thought that might help explain things. Ones that may not have occurred to you before.'

'You bet they haven't! But . . .'

'Oh, the wife's often the last to know.'

Pat heard the sound of heavy wheels crunching on gravel outside in the drive. With a glance at Callaway – for goodness' sake, he had her so well intimidated that she had almost felt she should ask his permission – Pat got up and looked out of the living-room window. Harold Harlan's Rolls was squeezing into a parking space, dwarfing her Mini and Callaway's modest saloon.

God, what a welcome sight. 'Excuse me a moment. It's a visitor, a friend,' she said, hoping that her feelings of relief were not too obvious.

'Of course.'

Once Pat was out of the room, Callaway rose briefly, went over to the window to check on the new arrival, nodded to himself and resumed his seat.

'Hello, Pat, I've come to take you to lunch,' were Harlan's first words when she opened the door.

'Oh, Harold, thank you,' Pat said with genuine pleasure, ushering him through into the hall. 'Just what I need.' She grimaced. 'I've got the ever-charming Sergeant Callaway here at the moment. I gather you've already met?'

'Not by my choice, but, yes, we have,' Harlan muttered.

When Pat led him into the living room, he looked at the Special Branch man with fastidious distaste.

'Morning, Callaway.'

'Morning,' the sergeant said, without getting up from his chair.

'Not interrupting anything vital, am I?' Harlan said brusquely.

Callaway shrugged. 'I was just about to leave.'

Harlan smiled ferociously, one shark signalling to another that the prey was his for a while now.

'Good,' he continued. 'I was hoping you'd say that. I think that this lady could do with a little rest and recuperation.'

Callaway got wordlessly to his feet, sliding his precious note book into the inside pocket of his jacket, and stalked out with only the curtest of nods to Harlan. Pat accompanied him to the front door and opened it quickly.

'Just think about what I've said,' Callaway told her quietly before he stepped out. 'I'll be back sometime soon. Have a nice lunch, Mrs Brack.'

When she returned to the living room, Harlan was standing squarely, hands in his pockets, clearly angry and concerned to get something off his chest.

'Oh, Harold,' Pat began, hoping for some tenderness, consolation.

But Harlan was in no mood for comforting anyone.

'Right,' he said coldly. 'Before we eat, one thing. What I want to know – and am entitled to know – is: has Paul ever had any dealings with agents of the Soviet Union? And has he ever had any inclination, politically, in that direction? Think carefully, Pat . . .'

She sank into an armchair and put her head in her hands. After a while she released her face and stared up at him in desolation.

'God, not you, too?' she whispered.

Callaway collected Seymour from Waldegrave House and within half an hour, after a swift drive through country roads, they were back on the motorway, heading for Dorset once more.

'Brack's office was clean, and of course Harlan and everyone else looked as though butter wouldn't melt in their mouths. Thorny customer, though, Brack's boss,' Seymour said.

Callaway did not take his eyes from the road. 'Yeah. I

bumped into him at the house. He wasn't exactly glad to see me again, particularly as he was whisking Brack's wife off to a restaurant.'

'Anything useful from Mrs Brack before Harlan turned up?' Seymour asked.

'Not much. She and Brack may have their problems, but she's basically the loyal type. Pity –' Callaway sighed. 'Sometimes deserted wives are a good bet. More often than not, they're eager to slang the old man with anything they can dredge up.'

Seymour nodded. 'How did she react when you got on to the reds under the nuptial bed?'

'Couldn't believe it. Usual reaction . . .'

'Maybe she's justified in that.'

'Maybe.'

'You know,' Seymour said reflectively. 'I smell a rat. I don't know where it lives, but there's one in there somewhere. There are quite a few things that just don't fit.'

Callaway pulled out to pass a juggernaut. 'Brack broke the law,' he said, peering into his wing mirror. 'He knew what he was doing, and he'll get his come-uppance. What more do you want?'

'I don't know,' Seymour murmured. He changed the subject. 'So you say Fletcher's ready with the confirmation about the source of the offending material?'

'Yeah,' Callaway said. 'I phoned him before I went round to the Brack place in Oxford. Chapter and verse are waiting for us down in Heathbridge, no problem.'

'Then we'll see him before we finally grant Dr Brack his martyr's crown,' Seymour mused, as if thinking aloud. 'The wife and Harlan have closed ranks, so that leaves us with Fletcher. I believe he worked with Brack before the man left the AEA, and those seekers after truth are a bitchy lot. If you want the real dirt on a scientist, in my experience all you have to do is put a few well-chosen questions to a colleague. . . .'

It was mid-afternoon by the time they arrived in Heathbridge. They parked in the official section of the car park and found out that the inquiry was still in progress in the main hall. Seymour had a word with one of the officials, and then they settled down in an empty classroom to wait.

Brian Fletcher sat at his place on the applicants' side wearing an expression of supercilious confidence. George Spiking had come back today, and he was doing his best to fill the gap left by Brack, but his best wasn't good enough.

The miners' leader was on his feet at the moment, brandishing a copy of a morning newspaper.

'I read an account in the *Guardian* on my way here this morning,' he thundered. 'According to this report, Dr Fletcher told this inquiry that we should think of ourselves as a "mature society". That, frankly, astonishes me – as, I'm sure, it must astonish you, sir,' he declared, granting the inspector a smile of mock sympathy.

Justice Wilkinson remained impassive.

Spiking continued, unabashed. 'If what Dr Fletcher says is true, then why do magistrates, chief constables, and your learned colleagues in the Judiciary up and down this land raise their voices more raucously by the day on the "collapse of moral values" and the "breakdown of law and order"?' he said. 'There are many of us who feel that our society is on the brink of destabilization. We see an increasingly centralized and authoritarian government machine trying ever more desperately to control groups of people who either resent or do not recognize their authority. Those, with respect, sir, are not signs of maturity – and to use that illusion to justify taking risks that are all too demonstrably real is behaviour worthy only of an ostrich.'

Fletcher noticed that Spiking's harangue brought murmurs of approval, even some applause, from the public seats. Let him: it was pure rabble-rousing. The man was probably rehearsing for the time when he would become a Tribunite MP. What he didn't have were facts. . . .

'These are the reasons why I point out,' Spiking concluded, 'that until Dr Brack has been formally charged with an offence, the subject he was attempting to discuss last week is not yet *sub judice* . . .'

The Inspector glared at him over the tops of half-moon glasses. 'Mr Spiking, I hope you are not attempting to reverse my ruling of yesterday?'

'I'm asking you to qualify it, Your Honour. Dr Brack was attempting to show how our society is increasingly vulnerable to attack by nuclear terrorists. That is a matter of the most immediate concern to the people of Heath-bridge. Although the reactor here – if it were built – would be safely sited away from the metropolitan area, it could never be made entirely invulnerable to organized terrorist attack. And if an attempt were made to hold central government to ransom, it would be the innocent people of this town who would be the meat in the sandwich. . . .'

An official tip-toed carefully to Fletcher's side and whispered a few words in his ear. As Fletcher left the hall, he heard another rumble of approval from the audience for George Spiking. The man was scoring his demagogic points, but they wouldn't bring Brack back, and there was no way Justice Wilkinson was going to change his ruling, he thought with quiet satisfaction.

The Special Branch men were waiting in a class room close to the hall, the sergeant who had arrested Brack and an urbane-looking type who seemed to be his superior.

'Dr Fletcher?' the senior man said pleasantly, offering his hand. 'Chief Inspector Seymour. You and Sergeant Callaway know each other . . .'

Fletcher nodded acknowledgement to Callaway and sat on a desk facing them. It was good to talk to a senior man: the young Special Branch man always looked ready to plant a half brick in your pocket – or maybe his fist in your face.

'Sorry to drag you out,' Seymour began.

'My pleasure!' Fletcher said with a rueful smile. 'This tedious pantomime seems to be going on for ever.' They were waiting expectantly, so he opened his briefcase and took out a sheet of paper. 'I've checked the source of

Brack's little outburst,' he said. 'It was a paper written in 1972 by a man who was then the project leader for research into laser enrichment, Simon Clarke. Unfortunately, he has since left the authority to work for Westinghouse in the States. Brack's pamphlet simply reproduces Clarke's general statements verbatim . . .'

'Hum . . . '72 . . .' Seymour mused. 'That makes it pretty old stuff. How does that affect its classification?'

Fletcher handed the typewritten summary to him. 'Still definitely Most Secret,' he said confidently. 'The point is, as Brack himself was at pains to point out, that if anyone masters that particular technology, then the Nuclear Non-Proliferation Treaty won't be worth its paper.'

Callaway was already making notes on the summary. 'And Brack would know all of that?' Seymour asked.

'Oh, yes!'

Seymour raised an eyebrow. 'We have most of the background material on Dr Brack,' he said. 'But perhaps you might be able to fill in a few details. Do take a seat,' he invited, motioning Fletcher to a chair strategically placed between him and Callaway.

Fletcher slid off the desk and sat down.

'So you knew Brack when he was working for the AEA?' Seymour said.

'Yes. We were both part of the team working on fusion technology. That's . . .'

'. . . The so-called "ultimate energy solution",' Seymour finished for him.

'More or less,' Fletcher agreed, slightly disconcerted. This copper had done his homework, or maybe he actually read books. 'Even after Brack broke with the authority and went to work for Harlan International, he did a stint for them debriefing Tchenkov, the Russian fusion expert who defected. Typically, Brack flounced out in disgust when things got politically thorny. I took over and went to the States to see Tchenkov, who had been carted off to Princeton. . . .'

'Quite,' Seymour interrupted. 'But I'm interested in Dr

Brack, and the precise reasons why he should have taken the actions he did. Now, he's just had something of a success with this book. It will have enhanced his reputation in many ways, even put him in a position of some considerable influence. And yet he goes and commits a very serious offence, quite deliberately.' Seymour's expression was shrewd. 'Why do you think he's done it?' he asked gently.

Fletcher paused. 'I don't know . . .' Then he changed his mind. 'There's maybe one reason,' he said. '*The Brack Report* may have attracted a lot of publicity, but professionally, in a very small but select area . . . well, he's put himself in a bit of a corner.'

'You mean, where does he go from here?'

'He has, in fact, blackballed himself from the field in which he originally made his career.'

'Nevertheless, supposing that to be true, the kind of notoriety that he is now attracting would hardly fit his needs,' Seymour said doubtfully.

'He's a very complex character,' Fletcher said, looking faintly aggrieved, as if he resented having his judgement questioned by a mere policeman.

Callaway raised his eyes to heaven. 'Complex character, my arse . . .' he muttered. But Seymour pressed on with smooth equanimity.

'Then do you think his behaviour has any political implications?'

'Well, you know what Andrei Sakharov says about Western anti-nuclear people?' Fletcher said, warming to one of his favourite themes. Seymour gestured for him to continue. 'Sakharov says that any destabilization of Western energy supplies is in the best interests of the Soviet Union. We have a clear lead over the Soviets in Fast Reactor technology – precisely the technology that Brack and others appear very anxious to torpedo.'

There was a savage bitterness in Fletcher's voice that Seymour noted with interest. His reaction was non-committal. 'And yet,' he said, 'I get the impression from others who know him that Brack is completely apolitical.'

Fletcher shrugged. 'It's just a thought that's crossed my mind from time to time. He's always been a radical thinker – which is, after all, good news and bad news. I'd be surprised if the habit stopped short of politics.'

Seymour said nothing. He glanced at Callaway, who had been staring sullenly round the room for the past few minutes, casting glances at his watch. The sergeant shook his head. No questions.

'Thank you, Dr Fletcher, anyway,' Seymour said smoothly, bringing the conversation to an end. 'Best of luck with your labours here. I don't envy you, I must say.'

'You have my phone number. I'll probably be with a friend . . .' Fletcher said.

'Certainly. We'll be in touch if necessary. Thanks again.'

When Fletcher had gone, Callaway said bluntly: 'Prat.'

His superior grinned. 'But at the moment he's our prat. And the evidence he's supplied is pretty conclusive on the face of it.'

'Yeah,' Callaway agreed. 'We shouldn't have any trouble making it stick. And that's our job, isn't it?'

The sergeant was on his feet, jacket buttoned, straightening his trendy slim tie in the reflection of one of the classroom windows, looking every inch the fighting cock.

Seymour shook his head. 'I just wish it didn't seem all too good to be true, too straightforward,' he said, then walked over to the door. 'Come on, let's see your Dr Brack. He's been stewing nicely. Time to put him out of his agony.'

Thirty hours after his arrest, Paul Brack looked a good deal more crumpled and haggard. If the isolation and uncertainty of the past day and a half had marked his appearance, he had nevertheless lost little of his natural taste for combat – as Seymour and Callaway found out to their cost. They had expected him to be talkative, and he was, but contrition was not his line. Try as they might, they could not force him to do much more than discuss the iniquities of the Official Secrets Act. The inspector was adept at oblique methods of information gathering, cosy chats that revealed the chinks in a man's armour more effectively than any frontal assault. Which was why, twenty minutes into what was supposedly an intensive interrogation, he and Callaway were listening to a lecture on the career of Basil Braintree, Secretary of State for Energy.

'What are Braintree's qualifications?' Brack was saying. 'A public school education that stunted his emotional, and distorted his intellectual development; a dilettante's degree at Oxford and a reputation for hot air in the Union debates; a whizz-kid's career in television journalism that exalted him to the ranks of housewives' hero and thence to one of the safest Tory seats. All that was followed by a few years of sycophantic activity in the charmed circle of his future leader, and so into office. Now you tell me,' he said, beaming at the two Special Branch men. 'What qualifies him to judge past, present and future trends in nuclear technology?'

Callaway was beginning to find it difficult to control himself. He unfolded his arms and leaned forward threateningly. 'If you ask me, it's about time you answered a few questions instead of giving us lectures, Brack,' he began.

The inspector put one hand on Callaway's shoulder and pulled him gently back, then leaned over the table himself.

'The answer, I think,' he said softly, 'is that the minister relies on the best available technical advice, Dr Brack.'

Brack gave a short, rasping laugh of contempt. 'By that, I suppose you mean old Frank Sampson, his Permanent Secretary?'

'Sir Frank, and others,' Seymour said.

'He's the one who dictates the department's line, so you can ignore the underlings,' Brack answered. 'He's been Permanent Secretary to three successive ministers, and his prejudices have shaped the policies of every one of them. It's got nothing to do with technical factors, don't you see? Sampson's a civil servant, close to the top of the system. Everything about nuclear power is tailor-made to fit the preferences of the bureaucratic mind.' He held up one hand and counted on the fingers. 'Nuclear power involves vast expenditure of capital, which means kudos for all the professionals involved. It requires very little labour – perish the thought of having to involve too many human beings! And lastly it's the perfect centralized system, totally under government control . . .' Brack smiled sourly. 'If only it was safe; if only it worked; if only we could afford it; and if only it didn't stand an evens chance of destroying the world in which we live . . .'

Suddenly he stopped. Seymour raised a quizzical eyebrow. 'Something wrong, Dr Brack?'

'No, I just noticed that the sergeant was taking notes. I wanted to make sure that he was able to keep up. I hate to be misquoted.'

Callaway nodded impassively. 'No problem. I know short-hand.'

'If, Dr Brack, you wish to think of us as mindless secret policemen, feel free,' Seymour said, with a hint of steel in his voice. 'I am aware that you have had a tough, lonely time these past thirty-odd hours, and I make allowances. But Sergeant Callaway has been taking notes because what you say seems relevant to the case. It is, after all, germane to the alleged offence that you feel that you are better equipped to decide what is in the national interest than the politicians or the civil servants – even, it appears, than parliament itself.'

Brack shrugged. 'Have you ever really listened to the level of parliamentary debate? MPs have no access to the facts either. They're kept as ignorant as the people they represent – and they come under the jurisdiction of the Official Secrets Act, too. . . .'

Seymour looked at him in exasperation. 'Itself passed by parliament,' he reminded him. 'Whatever you, Dr Brack, may think of the Act, it has been on the Statute Book for almost three-quarters of a century. And although there have been half-hearted moves by some members of parliament to amend it, it is still there. Its purpose is to protect the state from those who wish to harm its interests – the "enemy within", to use a slightly melodramatic phrase. It does that,' he added, watching Brack carefully for a reaction, 'by putting individual offenders in prison for extremely long terms.'

Brack nodded, as if Seymour were simply stating the obvious. The Special Branch officer had no choice but to press on, though he changed his tack slightly.

'That being the case,' he said, 'if your purpose is to fight a crusade against the Act you will be severely impeded by the restrictions of a maximum-security prison. You have a family, Dr Brack, and a brilliant reputation. You would be well advised to answer some of my questions, so that, together, we can explore any alternatives, look for circumstances that might make such a course unnecessary. . . .'

Brack seemed slightly subdued by the inspector's new line. He gazed around the bare interview room, then down at his own shabby, crumpled suit. 'I'm pretty clear about the stick, thanks,' he said. 'Less so regarding the carrot. In fact, I can't conceive what you might have in mind, inspector.'

'It may sound old-fashioned to say so,' Seymour ventured, 'but we do live in a democratic society. We have already spoken about parliament. Did you, for instance, ever raise this matter with your constituency MP?'

Brack's more sober mood collapsed in the face of that question. He threw his head back and laughed.

'Oh, yes,' he said after a while, 'I went to see an MP, at the House of Commons. He was very nervous about the possibility of our conversation being overheard – and I mean concerned for himself, because he thought *I* might be bugged in some way, that *I* might incriminate him if he were to say something indiscreet! When we finally got ourselves into a private room, he warned of the possible damage such ideas could do to my professional career.'

'This was while you were still an employee of the Atomic Energy Authority?' Seymour asked quickly, with a warning glance at Callaway to his right.

Brack smiled. 'To that question, no comment until I've been allowed to see my solicitor.' Then he picked up his thread again. 'Anyway, to continue, he told me that he was powerless to raise the issue in the House because it was subject to "D" notice restrictions.'

He paused and looked at Callaway, who was taking notes with redoubled urgency. 'For the record,' Brack drawled. 'I'm not naming the MP, but I can tell you that he wasn't actually my constituency MP, just one I thought might be sympathetic. Got that?'

Callaway looked up, glowering, then carried on writing.

There was a moment's silence before Brack shifted his attention back to Seymour.

'So where do you suggest that I might have taken the matter from there? To the ombudsman?' he asked, his voice heavy with sarcasm.

Seymour refused to give in. He smiled urbanely. 'Did you then, ever attempt to raise the question of secrecy with your superiors at the Atomic Energy Authority during your period of service there?'

Brack grinned back at him and wagged an admonitory finger. 'As I said: no comment. It seems to me that you have a lot of file browsing to do yet, inspector.'

'Is it, then, your absolute determination to refuse to help me?' Seymour said. 'Do you not wish to mitigate the seriousness of your situation in any way? Your predicament . . .'

'I see no predicament, or at least not as you, with respect, would understand it.'

Seymour gazed at him unhappily. Where he should have felt irritation at the man's gall, he felt only a vague unease. Given more time, he might get through to Brack, but time was something he did not have. Soon they would have to get a committal or release him. And the *prima facie* case was so strong that he would not be doing his job if he didn't get that committal.

'I take it, in that case, that you agree that you took the action you did of your own free will, as a matter of unchangeable principle, and furthermore in full knowledge of the consequences that would flow from it?'

Brack nodded. 'Why deny it? Your policeman heard what I said at the inquiry hall. What's done is done.'

Seymour braced himself. 'Then I have no alternative, Dr Brack, but to charge you formally with an offence under Section Two of the Official Secrets Act.'

11

Brian Fletcher drew the cork from the château-bottled claret and poured wine into two glasses. He glanced round and saw that Sarah was already at the table in the middle of her living room, helping herself to some pâté with the solitary concentration of someone eating alone in a familiar restaurant. Prospects for the planned reconciliation dinner did not look too promising.

He walked over and put her glass down by her plate before taking a seat himself.

'Thanks. Cheers,' Sarah said grudgingly, without looking up.

Fletcher realized that he needed to clear the air right now. He reached over and stayed her hand.

'Darling,' he said pleadingly. 'Let's not fall out over Paul tonight, eh?'

Sarah put her glass down heavily. Her eyes were defiant and hard.

'We seem to disagree over basic matters of principle. That's serious for people as involved with each other as we're supposed to be, don't you think? Tell me, do you want Paul to end up in jail?'

Fletcher laughed self-consciously and shook his head. 'Of course not, love,' he said. 'I wouldn't wish that on anyone – and particularly not on a former colleague for whom I still have considerable respect.'

'That's not how you were talking a couple of days ago.'

'He was putting me under a lot of pressure, Sarah,'

Fletcher said. 'Let's drink to his release,' he said, raising his glass.

'You don't mean that,' Sarah said sullenly.

He replied with a long-suffering sigh. 'Would I say it if I didn't?'

'To keep me happy for a while, yes. . . .'

'Darling, please,' Fletcher said. 'Let's enjoy the meal. Come on – let's drink to Paul out of clink.'

If he was making an impression, it hadn't started to show yet. Sarah took a drink, but with no more enthusiasm than before.

'Well, that's one psychological hurdle over,' Fletcher said heartily. Her eyes told him: speak for yourself. But he persisted with the next stage. 'Look,' he began. 'There's something regarding matters of principle that needs saying, but it's difficult without sounding patronizing.'

'Perhaps that's because it probably is,' Sarah retorted with soft venom.

'No, it's not,' Fletcher said. 'You know, one of the things I really love about you is the way you've held fast to your marvellously romantic view of science.' He ignored her pout and pressed on. 'I suppose it's your background – your father, of course, but also the whole atmosphere you grew up in. You were nurtured on attitudes that hadn't changed since the nineteenth century, when science was a gentleman's pastime, the pure, unsullied search after truth. Of course, there were still unsavoury elements of personal pride involved, but at least in those days they weren't affected by pressures from industry and politics. I think because you were born rich, because you don't have to do the work you do, you've inherited that attitude.'

Sarah snorted sceptically. 'I don't think it's got anything to do with my background,' she answered, toying with the remains of the pâté on her plate. 'At least, I hope not. And Paul Brack's father, as I recall, was a bricklayer in Huddersfield.'

Fletcher's smile was indulgent and expansive, without a trace of his usual resentment when Brack's name was mentioned. 'Well, I'm envious. It's a great attitude if you can afford it.'

'Science has never needed its independence more,' Sarah said stubbornly. 'The trouble is that the state pays fat salaries, and it demands its price.'

'Darling,' Fletcher chuckled. 'Even you can't afford to build a Torus in your back yard.' He leaned forward earnestly. 'Things are different these days. It's grown up, and like every adult it has to make compromises. We have to accept that government and private interests finance our research – and, to a certain extent, the piper calls the tune. It's as true of Paul as it is of the rest of us,' he said sagely. 'After all, where do you think Harold Harlan gets his financial backing?'

The last point hit its mark. Sarah frowned for a moment, then couldn't help smiling.

'I'm sorry,' she said, with more warmth than she had shown for some days past. 'I suppose for the moment we'll have to agree to disagree.'

Brian took her hand. 'I'm sorry, too, love, as a matter of fact. This whole thing's a rotten mess.'

After that, the atmosphere cleared considerably. Brian insisted on fetching the main course from the oven, and they ate with a will, discussing the inquiry and the problem of Brack without rancour.

'Do you really think Paul could be in big trouble over the material he published about laser enrichment?' Sarah asked.

'Ah . . . maybe . . .' Fletcher muttered, caught off his guard. Then he laid down his knife and fork and leaned back in his chair. Might as well come out with it while things were good between them. 'Well, yes, actually, I think he could be,' he admitted. 'The Special Branch chaps asked me to check it out – being the chief AEA man there, you understand – and it turned out that Paul had quoted whole sections from a confidential report prepared some years back by Simon Clarke – before your time, I think. I don't even know where he is now.'

At that moment the telephone rang. Fletcher went to get it, grateful for the respite. He came back after a couple of minutes, looking both sheepish and oddly aggressive.

'Who was that?' Sarah said.

Fletcher sighed. 'Actually, it was the police,' he said carefully. 'I'm afraid Paul's been charged. An hour or two ago. He seems to be making no attempt to evade the consequences.'

Sarah slowly put down her forkful of Chicken Marengo. The atmosphere was suddenly sub-zero again.

'I'm sorry . . .' Fletcher said defensively. 'There's no need to look at me like that.'

'That's all right,' Sarah murmured. 'It's just that I hadn't quite expected . . . Brian, I think I'm going to need some time alone, away from things. . . .'

Alan Stevenson's practised remand-cell technique was holding up – with difficulty.

'Dr Brack,' he said patiently. 'I really would advise you to say as little as possible under these circumstances. Baiting the Special Branch is not the cleverest thing you could do. When you understand that, you'll make my task a lot easier.'

'And, perhaps, theirs,' Brack said. The sliding window in the cell door opened briefly, an eye appeared, then it snapped shut. 'They do, after all, seem to have things mostly their own way, I think you'll agree,' he added, motioning towards the door.

Stevenson shook his head. 'I'm just trying to advise you on the basis of my own experience in these cases,' he answered mildly.

'All right,' Brack conceded. 'Then I suppose I'd better listen.' He had some shaving things and writing materials now that he had been formally charged, but his surroundings hadn't changed, and neither had the crumpled feel of the clothes he was sitting in – the same he had been wearing when he had been arrested three days before. The prosperous, pin-striped solicitor had the air of one of those eighteenth-century gents visiting the madmen in Bedlam – except that he clearly wasn't here for his own amusement.

'Yes, please do,' Stevenson said. 'As far as I'm concerned, the moral, social, scientific – or any other – grounds on which you took the action for which you have been charged are a very secondary consideration. My job consists of preparing a defence in law against a serious . . . alleged . . . offence,' he said carefully. 'And the first step is to secure for you the maximum personal freedom of action while that defence is being prepared.'

Brack rested his elbows on the bare table between them. 'As regards the . . . as you say, alleged . . . offence,' he said with a tight smile. 'Let me tell you one thing. If the authorities really tried hard, they could make a case against almost any scientist who's ever worked for them. Speak to anyone at the AEA about the Official Secrets Act, and they'll tell you the truth: that it's an ugly, blunt instrument which is there as a permanent threat, to be used against anyone who steps too far out of line . . .'

'I am well aware of that fact,' Stevenson replied grimly. 'But that, I would submit, is something we can discuss later, when the situation calls for it. The law may be an ass, Dr Brack. Personally, I would agree with you on this particular area of legislation. From a practical point of view, however, the reality is that the authorities are taking it very seriously indeed. When you get out of here, you will find that other people – including your family and Harold – have also learned just how seriously. Now,' he said, staring hard at Brack, 'could we discuss the first step I mentioned?'

Brack nodded dumbly. 'Are Pat and the kids okay?' he said.

'Bloody but unbowed is the phrase, I think,' Stevenson answered. 'The same goes for Harold, though I gather he's having to make a lot of reassuring calls to his investors. In between times, he also seems to have found time to visit your wife, I might add, and do what he can.'

The solicitor's point hit home, as it was meant to.

'All right, then,' Brack said. 'I won't make things more difficult than they already are.'

'Good. I shall be trying for bail at the committal proceedings tomorrow morning.'

'And the chances?'

Stevenson pursed his lips. 'Not bad, on the whole,' he said. 'The Crown will probably make sure the sureties are stiff, but it's not as if you're actually Klaus Fuchs, atom spy – or, for that matter, Jack the Ripper.'

'Nice to be reassured,' Brack said wryly, with a touch of his old spirit.

'Yes, but don't think they're going to keep the kid gloves on when it comes to your trial. Speaking personally, I'd say someone up there wants you put away. They'll be using every weapon they've got – and Harold knows that. He'll put up bail, but he'll make sure you play things his way now that you've made your point.'

Brack nodded slowly. 'I suppose he must have his pound of flesh,' he mused, rising to his feet as Stevenson closed his briefcase with an air of finality.

The smile on the solicitor's face was bland, but his words were waspish. 'He's sticking his neck out for you, Dr Brack,' he said. 'And I think we could carve off a hefty portion of your body tissue without putting things even. Inconceivable as it may seem, I'm starting to suspect that Harold Harlan actually likes you.'

Sarah Challen drove her sports car fast through the winding Berkshire lanes towards Harwell, with all the skill and precision that came from years of driving a finely tuned, responsive machine. The Lotus ate up the miles: she made it to her step-father's house in less than half an hour.

Norman Phillips was out on the terrace, enjoying the fine day – if that was the right word to express his feelings. Sarah's phone call earlier in the day had established that her mother had gone to London on a shopping trip, and

Phillips had tried to put her off from driving over. As he greeted her, trying to put on a cheerful, paternal face, he betrayed himself as a troubled man, who badly needed time to think. Sarah, however, had already decided to be merciless with him. Even while he was getting her a drink, she came out with her question about the authority's – and his – attitude towards the prosecution of Paul Brack.

'There's no victimization,' Phillips said, handing her a Perrier water with a twist of lemon. He frowned thoughtfully. 'At least not as far as I know. But I must admit that I can't understand what game Paul thinks he's playing.'

'"Game" is hardly the word, is it?' Sarah interrupted.

Phillips beckoned for her to follow him in through the french windows and sat down wearily in a chair in the large, expensively decorated living room. 'Do you know, I think it is as far as he's concerned?' he said. 'That's what I've found most difficult to take about him. An uneasy feeling that . . . that he's playing with me.'

Sarah stared at her step-father with new interest. She had not seen much of her real father, Maxwell Challen, as a child; the divorce and her mother's remarriage to Phillips had happened when she was hardly old enough to understand, and to all intents and purposes this man had brought her up. She had not picked up her relationship with Maxwell Challen until she was in her teens and already intending to enter scientific research. All the time, Norman Phillips had stood for commitment to nuclear power, absolutely and unconditionally, and he had exuded quiet self-confidence. Now this self-doubt. . . . She motioned for him to continue.

Phillips, however, merely shrugged. 'What *does* Paul want now?' he asked. 'You probably have more idea than I.'

Sarah winced inwardly at the implications of his assumption. The pain of having Brack and then losing him was still there. 'I think . . . and I can only assume it, because I haven't seen him for a while . . . that he believes *The Brack*

Report has established an irrefutable case, and that if he can draw the attention of enough people to it, they will accept its inexorable logic and force the politicians to act.'

Phillips shook his head in mute despair. Twenty years of dealing with men of power had taught him that 'irrefutable logic' played a very small part in getting things done.

'Whatever happened to you two?' he said gently. 'I thought you might have been able to focus his talent.'

'Oh, I tried,' Sarah admitted. 'When he was with the AEA, even afterwards, but there was never much chance of that.' She changed the subject quickly. 'Are they going to prosecute?'

Phillips nodded. 'Braintree thinks it provides an excellent opportunity to keep him away from Heathbridge. Whether or not they go the whole way with it depends on whether they believe they have a case.'

'What do you think?'

'Well, he's done his best to hand it to them on a plate.'

Again Sarah said nothing, simply waited for her step-father to go on.

'You know,' he said after some thought. 'I've always wanted to hold on to Paul – to harness him, I suppose. I know he despises me intellectually, and I wish he wouldn't do that, because it makes things a lot harder for me.' Phillips's voice was thick with emotion. 'It's a very difficult thing to have to accept – eventually, after you've fought and resisted his arguments for years, that the bloody man has been right all along.'

'You're not accepting *The Brack Report*?' Sarah said incredulously.

'Good heavens, no!' Phillips answered. He went over to the drinks table and poured himself another gin and tonic. Sarah shook her head when he asked if she wanted anything stronger. She needed to keep a clear mind.

When Phillips sat down again his sallow, almost cadaverous features were solemn. 'But . . .' he said. 'There's always a "but", isn't there? I mean, I thought for years he was overstating the inherent problem of on-load refuelling in the AGR. Fifteen years later, I'm eating humble pie. I resisted his interpretation of what had happened to the core of the Wintersham reactor in the earthquake. And here we are, two years later, and the damned thing is still not back in commission.' He took a stiff drink from his glass, and suddenly Sarah thought he looked old and tired. 'Almost everybody – with the honourable exception of yourself,' he continued, 'derided his theoretical alternatives to the official line on fusion research. Then Tchenkov drops into our lap and proves him right. The man is, though I hate to say it, an original. He's impossible to contain, or control, he's as objectionable and arrogant as all hell at times. But the fact has to be faced that he is . . . I don't know . . . a visionary . . .'

'Whom the State, in its infinite wisdom, will now do its damnedest to incarcerate for twenty years?'

Phillips winced. 'Innovation is extremely painful in a hierarchical society like ours. We all take refuge in our little empires, and who needs to be told they're built on sand? Change hurts, both for the innovator and for the man he's trying to challenge.' He looked at his step-daughter for a spark of sympathy, found none, and turned away, unable to look her in the eye. 'Oh, Sarah,' he sighed. 'Have we got problems!' After a few moments he looked back at her appealingly. 'But how can any human being admit that Brack has a solution when he behaves like this?'

'Perhaps no one can,' Sarah said slowly. 'But I want to help him stay at liberty to change things. And what I want from you at the moment is a little rule-bending, because I intend to find a man named Simon Clarke.'

The police convoy, sirens shrieking, was forced to slow down until the units stationed outside the magistrates' court managed to clear a pathway. In the back of the leading car, Seymour and Callaway sat hunched over some papers. Callaway glanced briefly out of the window at the two or three hundred demonstrators milling around in the narrow street. He read the banners: 'FREE BRACK', HEATHBRIDGE-HIROSHIMA', 'REPEAL THE OFFICIAL SECRETS ACT'. His face expressed no sympathy. Unlike Seymour, he'd done his spell on the beat during the mushrooming of political demonstrations in the early 1970s, and he didn't care what they were protesting about any more, just remembered all those Sundays worked and double-shifts.

'Good turn-out for a weekday.' he growled. 'Haven't they got jobs to go to?'

He turned back to the chief inspector, flipping a photograph out of one of the files he had been showing him. Callaway was nothing if not an assiduous collector of information. Seymour looked at the picture, then at the sergeant: it was a shot from a local newspaper and featured a handsome middle-aged lady pinning a rosette on a huge Hereford bull.

'I recognize the lady,' he said. 'It's the very worthy mayor of Heathbridge. But I don't quite get the relevance of her fat friend. . . .'

Callaway pointed to the man holding the bull's halter and smiling proudly into camera.

'Never mind the ruddy beef mountain. The fellow there is Mr George Frimley, local gentleman farmer and chairman of the magistrates here. Mrs Minchin is the anti-nuclear leader . . . get the point? You know what these county mafias are like.' He tapped his nose meaningfully. 'Seems to me that the sooner we get the committal over, on whatever terms, and move the whole thing down to London, the better.'

Seymour stroked his chin thoughtfully. He knew Callaway was aching to get back to the big city; that was his element, where he felt safe.

'I don't know, though,' he murmured. 'London would provide Brack with an even bigger gallery to play to. And that may be what he's after.'

The police had brought in reinforcements and had succeeded in clearing a passage for the convoy.

'Seems to me,' Callaway said, glancing at the skirmishes going on all round the cars, 'he's got all the attention he needs here – and more.'

Seymour nodded, conceding the point. 'Yes. I think I have one or two people to see in London, anyway.'

'With your permission, I'd like to telex the States and check through the computers,' Callaway said quickly.

'Oh?'

'I'd feel better if I knew a bit more about the bloke who wrote that paper Fletcher unearthed. All right?'

Seymour chuckled. 'Be my guest. But don't think the Branch will send you off to America expenses-paid. There's a recession on, you know. We're supposed to be cutting public spending.'

Their car drew to a halt outside the side door of the court building. Seymour and Callaway got out quickly and were forced to stand by while the uniformed PC in the back of the second car tried to persuade Brack to have a blanket draped over his head. They watched, hovering protectively, as the scientist shook his head emphatically and finally got out, blanketless, head held erect. Seymour heard Brack say in a loud, cheerful voice: 'What have I got to be ashamed of?' He waved to the crowd before being bundled through the double doors and into the womb of the building.

Harlan sat in front of the television set in his flat, pre-lunch scotch in his hand, Sophie Ferris by his side. He watched in sour silence, first film of Brack waving outside the court, then the summing up from Nick Rowe of ITN:

'Reporting restrictions were not lifted, and the hearing was held in camera at the request of the police. The magistrate, Mr George Frimley, remanded Brack for fourteen days, but saw fit to grant bail in the massive surety of a quarter of a million pounds put up by Brack's employer, Mr Harold Harlan of Harlan International Energy Consultants . . .'

Sophie smiled. Alan Stevenson had phoned straight after the hearing, but it was good to see the pictures. 'I always thought you were an old softy underneath, Harold,' she teased.

Harlan grunted. 'Balls,' he said. 'I'm gambling on the fact that someone up there likes the man. And I'm protecting my investment . . . from himself.'

12

Pat Brack parked her Mini as close as possible to the flats and she and Paul got out and hurried inside. The press hadn't arrived here yet, but there was every chance they would soon.

The shock came the moment that Brack opened the door and stepped through. Pat saw her husband tense, and moved forward to his side.

'Oh, God,' she said.

There were files and papers all over the floor and the desk. Drawers had been pulled open and their contents tipped out. Even the collection of back numbers of *Scientific American* that Brack kept on the top of his bookcase had been scattered around.

Brack strode over to his desk and began leafing through the papers strewn on its surface. He looked up at the space on the wall above his typewriter where he had pinned the excerpt from Maxwell Challen's Oxford Union lecture, grimaced and reached over to open the sash window. He stayed at the open window with his back to Pat for several moments, as if he needed to breathe the clean, unsullied air.

Pat took a pace forward and stood staring around the room in horror. 'I can't believe this,' she whispered.

Brack turned away from the window. 'Reality is always harder to take than fiction.' He began to pick up papers from the floor and pile them on the desk, ready for sorting. 'Why don't you put the kettle on?' he said quietly.

Pat knelt to retrieve a paperweight that had been tossed on to the carpet. She put it back in its place by the typewriter, looked around hopelessly and said: 'Let's leave it, Paul. Just leave it and go home.'

Her husband stopped clearing up and met her gaze. A moment of fleeting sadness, then he smiled. 'Thank you.'

'But . . .?'

'I have to report to Waldegrave police station every day – to prove I'm still a sitting duck.'

He knew the meaning of the invitation, Pat thought. And he was grateful, in his way. She would press him a little, not too hard.

'We could change that to Oxford – it's a technicality,' she said, trying to sound light.

Brack shook his head with an air of finality. 'Harold, who for some extraordinary reason thinks I'm worth a quarter of one of his millions, is expecting me in the morning at Waldegrave House. I owe him that. You were going to bring the kids over for lunch, once I'd done my duty.'

They carried on tidying the place together, speaking little, neither willing to risk touching the other's fragile feelings. Brack would occasionally find something particularly significant had been removed, and he would mention the fact in a bland voice, like an announcer giving sports results, building up a checklist of violated possessions.

'It's frightening, isn't it?' Pat said after a while, not sure what she was referring to – themselves or the world they were living in. 'One can go on in what's laughably called normality. Then . . . how easily one can tear the tissue-thin surface . . . the mere skin of our being. When that happens, how incoherent, how utterly incomprehensible, suddenly, appear the parts . . . the framework over which we somehow contrive to stretch that skin . . .'

She thought she saw her husband incline his head, but then he went to fill the kettle. She watched him through the open kitchen door, and decided he hadn't wanted to hear.

'I don't know how you feel,' she sighed. 'But I'm shattered.'

Brack came to the door. He looked pale, but his eyes were bright.

'Good,' he answered baldly. He swept his arm out, in a gesture that embraced both of them as well as the sad chaos of the room.

'As we pick up the pieces,' he continued, 'we'll take a fresh look at them. And be less fooled by the skin.'

He smiled almost shyly and went back into the kitchen to make the coffee.

When they had managed to restore a semblance of order, Pat went out shopping, leaving her husband to work on the finishing touches. She had been to the flat only rarely, occasionally coming in when picking up or setting down the children here, and it felt strange to know that this was his – what was the awful American phrase? – his 'space', which he controlled absolutely.

Brack was at the piano when she returned from her expedition down the village high street, and she left him in peace, listening as she unpacked the groceries and stowed them in the fridge and cupboards, unable to resist tidying there, too, and throwing away occasional pieces of food of doubtful age and quality. She had bought some flowers at a stall by the station, which she was forced to arrange in a jug for want of a vase.

The piece he was playing was Bach, a composer whose combination of mathematical precision and sudden visionary leaps had always appealed to Paul. He claimed that Bach had achieved what most scientists had never even tried, and he was only half joking.

Pat nodded her appreciation as he finished playing and looked up. Her husband's attachment to his piano was pure pleasure, without a hint of duty, and the result was one in which feeling shamelessly trampled on technique. There were times when she felt she could love him just for that one fact.

She placed the jug of flowers on the piano.

'Thank you.'

Pat smiled. 'The garden's full of them at home,' she said,

then realized that talk of home was futile. 'Good to hear that piece again,' she added quickly. 'I used to think I liked it because it was the only activity – apart from reading – that stopped you talking.' Brack laughed. 'But it's more than that,' she said.

Brack got up from the piano stool and made a great show of admiring the flowers. He could see that Pat was putting on her coat, but he did not turn for the moment.

'I must get back, Paul,' she announced, forcing him to face her.

He stood by the piano, arms hanging loosely by his sides, suddenly looking sad and helpless, despite the dutiful smile.

'I feel as though I mustn't say a word,' he said.

Pat put a finger to her lips. 'Then don't.' She began to move towards the door. 'Good luck with Harold tomorrow. Watch his demon right hook. And let me know by mid-day if it's all right to bring the kids.'

Brack took a step forward. 'Pat?' he said, his voice bleak and lost.

She came towards him, brushed his lips with hers, then broke and was gone before he could find any more words.

The suitcase full of papers and files taken from Brack's flat lay open on the table in the corner of Harold Harlan's office at Waldegrave House. He and Brack stood on either side of it, eyes blazing, like estranged parents rowing over the custody of a child.

'What I'd like to know,' Brack bellowed. 'Is why you thought it necessary to turn my flat inside out? And who the hell gave you the right to do it?'

Harlan, too, was pale with anger, but his voice had taken on a dangerous calm. 'Forget the crap about rights!' he said. 'I've had three divorces in my time, Paul. The first one cost me a fortune, the second only half, and the third hardly anything at all. It's called learning from mistakes.'

Brack refused to be mollified. Harlan broke the staring stalemate by subsiding into his chair.

'Look, Paul,' he said. 'When it comes to making a mess of my life I'm as good at it as anyone else. But I've learned to clean up before the vultures move in.' He fixed Brack with a level stare, keeping his anger in check. 'Let's say I thought it wise to give them as little material for insinuation and innuendo as possible. And you should be very glad I did, Paul, because this lot could've put you away for as long as Rudolf Hess. What the hell is it all about?' Harlan finished, patting the desk in exasperation.

'Didn't your legal experts advise you?' Brack retorted waspishly. 'They seem to have taken over our lives.'

Now, however, the anger was ebbing from both of them. Harlan stood up again, looking businesslike again. 'Don't be supercilious, Paul,' he sighed. 'The time is not right for that kind of self-indulgence.'

Harlan paused, waiting for Brack to say something more, and when that was not forthcoming reached over and picked up the excerpt from Challen's anti-nuclear lecture that Foster had taken from the flat in Waldegrave. He put the paper down on the desk in front of Brack.

'Tell me,' he said softly. 'Have you been speaking to Max Challen? Lately, I mean . . .'

Brack shrugged and said nothing.

'In that case,' Harlan continued. 'I shall have to say it again: Max has spent twenty years in the wilderness because he took the road you're thinking of taking now. He threw away a position of enormous influence in a moment of passionate idealism. Paul,' he pleaded with real passion in his voice, 'your Report has put us in a position where people are going to listen to what we have to say on the subject of energy policy. After its publication, the whole spectrum of alternative-strategy organizations – not just Harlan International – are going to be able to better bend the public ear. . . . On the other hand, if you're going to rant and rave like a latter-day John Wilkes from the dock of the Old Bailey on an obscure matter of principle, then you'll throw away everything that's been gained for what you believe in.'

'It's still a matter of persuasion,' Brack said stubbornly. 'The nuclear monster bestrides us like a Colossus. All right, that's a grandiose image, but it fits: the legs which support it are defence and energy. You have to sweep away both to topple it. There is a rising groundswell of concern that –'

Harlan cut in impatiently. 'You're a bright boy, Paul,' he snapped. 'But when it comes to describing what you think you can achieve, then grandiose is the right word, too. You cannot divide yourself. What you have to accept – painful though it may be – is that there are one or two other people around with talent and commitment, and that you have to rely on them to win the battles *they're* fighting. Because, God though you think you may be, you can't win them all!'

'But it's a logical development, Harold. An extension of the same problem . . .'

'To hell with development!' Harlan exclaimed. 'We've made the running on the energy issue, and now's the time to consolidate, build on what we have. Leave disarmament alone – that's a problem for someone else, and your Report will be good fuel for them.'

'But disarmament can help *us*,' Brack insisted.

Harlan got up again and began to pace around the room, his mouth set in a hard line of determination. Persuasion seemed to have failed: it was time to use the bludgeon. Suddenly he swung and faced Brack.

'Listen,' he said harshly. 'There's an American theory. It says that in the manufacture of any new high-technology product there comes a point when the production manager has to shoot the design engineer. On this issue, that point arrived when we published the Report. That,' he rasped, 'is when I should have shot you!'

A silence, chastened perhaps.

'Now, God knows why, but I've put up a lot of money to get you out on bail. And I can tell you – more than half my head tells me you'd be safer where you were.'

Brack laughed in derision. 'Oh, come on! You're not trying to tell me you've got a heart?'

Harlan made no answer to that, simply glared at Brack

and went on. 'But,' he said, 'since I have let you out, I'm putting you on a leash. Alan Stevenson's a good man, and I'm paying him handsomely for his advice. I want you to give him every possible assistance in the task of preparing a defence. And if you don't like the way he wants to play it, you can go back to prison tomorrow. Try changing the world from inside of Wormwood Scrubs, Paul.'

13

Sir Frank Sampson, Permanent Secretary to the Department of Energy, was more than slightly ruffled by Chief Inspector Seymour's visit. After all, one knew these chaps were busy with things, but one didn't expect them to come barging into one's office – particularly since that office was directly adjacent to that of a minister who thought everything was being dealt with quietly and far from his vulnerable empire.

Seymour, for his part, was enjoying the encounter. It was not very often that he had the chance to beard a senior civil servant in his lair.

'So far as the department is concerned,' Sampson said stiffly, 'Brack has simply committed an offence – which he has admitted – against the Official Secrets Act, which is a police matter pure and simple, as you must well know.'

The Special Branch man just stared at him, impassive and level. Sampson glanced at his watch: luckily the Secretary of State should be in the House for another half-hour yet. So long as this flatfoot didn't intend settling in for a long stay, the situation was retrievable.

'I really don't know why you're here,' he said. 'It's most improper, inspector.'

Seymour smiled easily and took his time to admire the Permanent Secretary's office. All this was far from the squalor of Special Branch's headquarters: new furniture, deep-pile carpets and eighteenth-century prints. It was fortunate that he had decided to let Sergeant Callaway mooch off on his own trail. These high-nesting birds like Sampson feathered their places well, and the surroundings would have deepened Callaway's class resentment to a new low.

'There's a rumour abroad,' he said suddenly. 'It suggests that there may be a political motive for this prosecution. I like to know where I stand, Sir Frank, and so I came to get an opinion from what I take to be the horse's mouth.'

'You have no right to make that assumption,' Sampson said pompously.

'Oh, it's just a simple precaution,' Seymour told him. 'Against being made to look like an omelette. You see, in the Branch our memories of the ABC trial are still sore. That particular fiasco started off with a big fanfare, too – and ended with a whimper. No one likes to look foolish.'

There was enough of a note of warning in Seymour's voice for the civil servant to swallow his pride. 'I think you'd better go on, inspector,' Sampson answered guardedly.

'Thank you, Sir Frank,' Seymour said. 'Now, two things bother me. Firstly, though I hold no brief for the anti-nuclear people, over the last four or five weeks a dispassionate observer could not help noticing that your side has lost quite a lot of points, and that the person scoring so freely against you is a man Joe Public has never heard of before – namely, one Dr Paul Brack. This Brack knows his onions, because he's a convert. Such names as St Paul and Thomas à Becket spring to mind, both men who changed sides and made a terrible nuisance of themselves to their former colleagues and superiors.'

Sampson nodded, chuckling at the comparison. 'Off the record,' he said, 'I'll say this. We were delighted when Brack made his eccentric outburst. I suppose it's even true to say we all knew it was on the cards.'

'We all' sounded very cosy, Seymour thought. But he smiled and said: 'And now that it's happened, you're happy to trust in the due process of the law?'

'Absolutely. Your second worry?'

Seymour had been looking forward to this one. 'Something rather different,' he said smoothly. 'The fact is, every step I've taken on Brack's trail so far, there's been someone else before me. Professional, too. Any idea who that might be?'

For a second the urbane mask dropped. Sampson glanced at the door that connected him with the minister's office and looked ready to panic. 'You mean . . .' he blustered.

'"Tidying up", we call it, and I think you understand the implications, Sir Frank. Not your people?' he asked comfortably, as if it were the most natural thing in the world.

'Certainly not!' Sampson barked, outrage overcoming fear.

Seymour smiled coldly, and his eyes did not leave Sampson's face. 'It's sometimes as necessary to hide evidence of innocence as it is of guilt. . . .'

'But that's an outrageous accusation –'

'It could be Moscow, then?' Seymour probed quickly.

'Good lord,' Sampson said. 'Is that a serious suggestion?'

Seymour remained impassive, savouring the Permanent Secretary's confusion. He did not like Sir Frank Sampson, and he had a strong feeling that at this man's behest his minister had bitten off rather more than he was going to be able to chew.

'Well, Sir Frank,' he said slowly, rising to leave, 'what do you think?'

Sarah Challen drove as fast as she dared up the winding, hilly road. She had eaten nothing since leaving home, and the last stretch into the mountains had really taken it out of her, but she kept going on nervous energy, raw, defiant excitement.

A crossroads. Sarah jammed the brakes on, glanced at the road map on the passenger seat beside her, then at an address scrawled on a piece of paper and pinned to the corner of the map with a paper clip. The names on the signpost were all incomprehensively Welsh – but, yes, *Llan* . . . well, whatever, was definitely the one.

The road she needed to take was a very minor one, unmetalled, snaking up through the forest and yet higher into the mountains. Sarah grimaced. If Norman Phillips and Maxwell Challen could see her now. Norman had given her the first clue, and her father had come up with the rest. Nothing like having a foot in both camps.

Sarah wrenched the wheel of the Lotus round to the right to accommodate the hair-pin turn, and the powerful sports car accelerated obediently up an incline that would have stalled lesser engines. The road amounted to little more than a track, badly maintained, with scrubby grass and weeds growing merrily down the middle. When these people decided to get lost, she thought wryly, they certainly did it in style.

The door of Harold Harlan's office at Waldegrave House opened, and he looked up enquiringly. It was Sophie Ferris, as he had thought.

'Well?' he said, cutting out the preliminaries. Sophie had driven up to tell him whether or not she had managed to arrange a meeting between him and Morgan Ellis. No phone calls – not with the Special Branch so tap-happy these days.

Sophie threw her fake-fur jacket over the back of the chair facing him and sat down, then made a face. 'It wasn't easy,' she said.

'Even for you?'

'Even for me,' she admitted with a pained smile. 'There was a time when Morgan was anxious enough to take *me* out to lunch, at least. So when I eventually tracked him down I asked why my charms had so suddenly faded.'

'And where did you track him down?'

Sophie shrugged. 'He'd only meet me at the House of

Commons – I felt he was trying to keep things as official as possible. Oh, he bent over backwards, introducing me to parliamentary colleagues – in my official capacity as your personal assistant. But he was looking over his shoulder all the time. . . .'

'Very unlike our fearless radical, don't you think? What's got into him?'

'Apparently he's been served with a 'D' Notice, which prevents him from talking on specific nuclear issues,' Sophie said. 'If it's any comfort, he told me – for old time's sake – that we were being investigated.'

Harlan laughed cynically. 'Well, *I* told *him* all about our friends Seymour and Callaway.'

'But that's not what he meant,' Sophie explained, almost in a whisper. 'He was talking about MI5.'

'Look, Dr Brack,' Alan Stevenson said. 'If it comes to a trial, you have some points to make – you wouldn't have done this otherwise. My job, on the other hand, is to help you prepare a case that will save you from prison. Can we discuss things on that basis?'

Brack thought for a moment, then nodded. This interview in his office had been at Harlan's insistence, but he had promised Harold he would co-operate and he would. In any case, it would help him get his own ideas clear. The last few days had hardly been conducive to sober, objective consideration of the issues.

Stevenson relaxed a little. 'Very well. You tell me what you want to air, what you're aiming to achieve, and I'll try to advise you how we can best do those things within the framework of the law.'

'Right,' Brack began. 'I made my gesture at Heathbridge because the conduct of the objectors' case was being reduced to the level of farce. I was prevented from pressing arguments home because the Inspector ruled that the facts were classified information under the Official Secrets Act. And,' he added firmly, 'I believe that to be a situation which no healthy society should tolerate and which, in our sick one, is accelerating the decay of our institutions.'

Stevenson, who had been jotting down some notes, looked up enquiringly. 'Was there, then, no way of making the point of the arguments without producing the actual facts, chapter and verse, so to speak?'

Brack leaned forward intently. 'No! Because then they turn round and attack the credibility of the argument because, they claim, it has no factual basis!'

'Damned if you do, damned if you don't,' Stevenson said.

'Precisely.' Brack smiled. 'I hate to do the Shakespeare game and quote from *Hamlet*, but there is indeed something very rotten here. Nuclear fission reactors have been funded for thirty years now on the basis of very high expectations,' he continued eagerly, warming to his theme. 'But they are highly sophisticated and almost impossible for government officials, even those with some scientific training, to monitor effectively. And they are contracted for on an open-ended cost-plus basis, which means the normal economic criteria don't apply. But development of the AGR – that's the Advanced Gas-Cooled Reactor, like the one proposed at Heathbridge – is still not complete. More and more money is being pumped in to get them right, with the result that vast amounts of our dwindling national capital are soaking away in self-perpetuating failures like Dungeness B, which is still unfinished after more than a decade. . . .'

'Which was why you felt the question to be urgent, presumably.'

'Who else but someone like me is going to be able to ask the right questions?' Brack said. 'Until we – the experts, if you like – can point to the facts of cases like this with impunity, the public whose money is being spent in such a profligate fashion can never be shown how their scarce resources are being wasted.'

The solicitor nodded bleakly. 'That all sounds very logical, and I'm sure it is, but it doesn't tell me why the

Special Branch have been asking questions about your loyalty.'

'I suppose because they think I'm another Klaus Fuchs after all!' Brack said with a nervous laugh.

'Have you any idea why they should seriously consider that possibility? Think carefully.'

'Perhaps disagreement with the established view amounts to disloyalty,' Brack said. 'In certain quarters, at least.'

Stevenson moved closer to what was, from his professional viewpoint, the core of the matter. He phrased his next question delicately.

'Can I take it that you haven't made any attempt to . . . ah . . . use your privileged information in foreign countries?' he asked.

Brack shook his head. 'I don't think so. It depends how you construe things. I corresponded with the Russian fusion expert, Tchenkov, for instance – with the knowledge of the AEA, then my employers. Of course, I suppose they might now turn round and say that was suspicious in itself. Secrecy bugs every scientist's life,' he said, then grinned. 'No pun intended, but apt nevertheless. As I said before, the Official Secrets Act is there as an invisible line. *They* can say you've crossed it, if it suits them, with the consequence that scientists in sensitive areas – and there are thousands of them – work in a climate of fear. You see, whenever the powers-that-be get worried about criticism, they tweak up the temperature a bit.'

'And why did you choose laser enrichment as the secret to blow, if that's the correct phrase?'

'Oh, it's the correct phrase, all right,' Brack agreed. 'I did it because during and after the Second World War an increasing amount of so-called "peaceful" scientific research was coming under the military umbrella, and thereby being included in the military rulebook, which says: obey orders and keep your mouth shut. And because ever since Eisenhower's "Atoms for Peace" programme in the fifties, which really got nuclear energy going, they've been promoting the fallacy that it's possible to proliferate nuclear power stations all over the place without increasing the risk of unofficial, unauthorized weapons construction.'

'You mean by terrorists?'

'Possibly. In any case, I think the people of Heathbridge have a right to know that the reactor that the dear old Central Electricity Generating Board, bless it, is proposing to build on their doorstep, could also be a prime military target, war or no war. And the horrifying thing is that there are some pretty crazy people about these days – with warped minds but a high standard of education. Soon they'll be able to build a bomb. All they'll have to do is to pinch some uranium from a lonely, laxly guarded military base – it's happened with other lethal weapons.'

'And you really saw no other way?' Stevenson asked vainly. He already knew the answer he would get.

'Under the circumstances, no. In a sense it wasn't a sudden decision. The Special Branch were very eager to know whether I had raised the secrecy issue when I worked for the AEA, and whether I took any what they would call political steps at that time. I admitted nothing – my protests are certainly on AEA records somewhere, and I would be surprised if other actions of mine are not filed along with them. Oh, I'd been thinking along these lines for years, but like most of my colleagues I lacked the final impulse to do something.'

'And so you did.'

'I did indeed,' Brack said. 'Which doesn't necessarily mean that I relish years in prison.'

Stevenson put down his pen and looked at Brack with the eyes of a man who faced defeat. Yes, it was all very logical, brave, moral, and perfectly argued. The trouble with Paul Brack's position was that it chose to ignore the fact that the state was stubborn and rigid, and that it would come down very heavily on him, logic or no logic. Unless something pretty dramatic and unexpected happened, it looked as though Brack was going to win the argument hands down – and end up in jail for as long as the authorities chose to put him there.

'Quite so, Dr Brack – Paul,' was all that Stevenson could find it in his heart to answer. Further comment seemed superfluous, even insulting.

14

The narrow lane turned into a rutted track, then finally petered out by a farm gate in a bog-like morass fed by the rains. There the Lotus had stuck fast, unable to move forward or back, until the hill farmer, who had seen Sarah Challen's predicament from the yard, had brought his battered tractor and a tow to pull her out.

Watched by a scattering of shaggy Welsh sheep, Sarah stayed in the driver's seat, looking demurely helpless, while the tractor hauled the car round in the thick mud. When the Lotus was back on the firmer surface of the lane and pointed downhill, the gum-booted farmer jumped down and silently unhitched the tow.

'I should keep to the main roads in future – such as they are,' he said laconically as Sarah got out to thank him. He was a well-built man in his late thirties, his face coloured by the outdoor life. The voice, though, was neither Welsh nor rustic but pure Oxbridge.

He turned to go, with a casual, dismissive wave of the hand.

'Thank you . . . Simon,' Sarah said.

The farmer stopped, faced her and looked at her in cold anger.

'I didn't think you were really lost,' he murmured. 'What are you, a journalist?'

'I . . . I didn't know how you'd take it . . .'

Simon Clarke moved back towards the tow. 'You're trespassing, madam,' he snapped, and hooked the car back on to the tractor.

Within moments he was up high in the driver's perch, throttling off down the lane again, staring straight ahead. Sarah's car slewed wildly as it careened along behind.

Taken by surprise, Sarah was forced to jump out of the way of the Lotus. Then she ran after Clarke, slipping in the wet grass by the side of the track, arms pumping, until she managed to catch up and draw alongside the tractor.

'You don't understand!' she panted, yelling to make herself heard above the roaring throb of the tractor's engine. 'I'm a friend of Paul – Paul Brack!'

Clarke glanced at her darkly, then put on the brakes and sat with the motor idling, waiting for her to elaborate.

She stood, mud on her cord jeans, hair blown up by the wind, and looked up at him in desperation.

'My name's Sarah. Sarah Challen,' she said quickly. 'And I need your help. Please . . .'

The man behind a hedge a hundred yards down the track watched with interest as Sarah Challen and Simon Clarke held a brief conversation, with her smart car still hanging bizarrely from the tractor's towing gear. When they walked off together in the direction of the low, slate-built farmhouse, he moved cautiously out of cover, his new gum boots squelching in the mud, and leaned up against a tree trunk with his hands in his anorak pockets. Sergeant Callaway had parked his saloon up a Forestry Commission road that ran off the lane, which in the event had proved wise policy, though it was going to be damp and chilly standing around in the open. He lit a cigarette and settled down reluctantly to wait. This capering around in the Welsh bloody mountains was not his style, he thought morosely. It had better be worth it . . .

The kitchen of the farmhouse had one of those stone floors that are very traditional and picturesque, but cold and unwelcoming in hard reality. As for the house's owner, Clarke had unfrozen a little, but was still very cagey. He said very little as he put some more wood on the open log fire and bustled around the low-ceilinged kitchen making coffee for the two of them. Only when she told him she was

Maxwell Challen's daughter, and explained the details of the Brack case, did he begin to show some openness. He was a man who had learned caution the hard way, Sarah judged, and the story he began to tell confirmed her suspicions – and more.

Clarke handed her the warming drink in a slightly misshapen glazed mug. The coffee was instant, and it tasted strongly of long-life milk, but she was grateful for it after the long trip from home.

He saw her look curiously at the mug, and he smiled fleetingly. 'There's a potter down the valley. She lets me have her failures for nothing. They hold the stuff, and they do me.'

They sipped in silence for a few moments, then Clarke spoke suddenly.

'Life here's all about innocence, I suppose,' he said. 'Paul Brack and I were all bright-eyed and naïve in the old days with the AEA, back in the early sixties – me particularly. The whole thing seemed the answer, positive, progressive, turning nuclear swords into ploughshares, all that hogwash. Oh, the nuclear establishment in this country's a nice, cosy place to be . . .'

Sarah nodded. 'Still is, if you don't think too much.'

'Sure,' Clarke said. 'It was only when I went to the States that the military-energy tie-up really hit me. The military-industrial complex, et cetera.' He shrugged. 'Where before the laser-enrichment thing had always seemed an interesting technical problem, it started to mean more over there. While I was working for Westinghouse, I became increasingly concerned about talk of a nuclear solution to the war in Vietnam. I got in touch with a group called Alternative Scientists in Boston, and through them I met Paul Brack again.'

'And did you talk to him about your fears regarding the applications of laser-enrichment technology?'

Clarke stared into his coffee, as if fighting to come to a decision, then looked up again at Sarah.

'It was he who felt I had to make a noise – to shock the

public into demanding some kind of action,' he said, in a neutral voice that held no malice and apportioned no blame.

'And . . .?'

'It was a possibility that had already crossed my mind. In the end I wrote a long article which was published in a small-circulation alternative science journal over there. That would be . . . I don't know, maybe six, seven years ago.'

Sarah felt a hot surge of excitement. 'This article . . . was it very detailed?'

'The whole caboodle – an A to Z of laser enrichment technology, bomb-making for beginners, I suppose.'

'And what was the response?'

Clarke's smile held no humour, only sadness and pain.

'Oh, the radical scientists thought it was marvellous. As for the rest, I'll give you the short version,' he said. 'Which is that I was fired by Westinghouse, blackballed in the nuke industry and everywhere else that's willing to pay for my kind of expertise. They broke up my marriage; tried to fix me on dope charges; committed me for psychiatric examination; finally they dumped me in Sydney and refused me re-entry to the States. That's when I picked up a few of the pieces and brought them back here.'

He looked at Sarah's appalled face. Perhaps he could sense the shame she was already feeling at her relief when he had told her about the article. There was nothing she could say, as Clarke well knew.

'*Voilà*,' he filled in for her. 'There you have dissident treatment – American style.'

'Oh God,' Sarah mumbled, then forced herself to go on. 'But . . . despite all that . . . you can help Paul. Are you willing?'

'If I can, yes,' Clarke said, putting his coffee cup on the hearth and rising to his feet. He ducked under the low door frame into the small living room of the farm house, where there were rough pine shelves lined with books, a desk and a battered filing-cabinet. 'Don't worry about me, Sarah,' he told her. 'You see, this innocence here is an illusion, because I know they can find me if they want to, just as you did. But I don't think they can harm me now. . . .'

Sarah quietly followed him through, into the sparsely furnished tomb of his dreams.

Seymour called at Sarah's flat in person to tell Brian Fletcher about Callaway's phone call from Wales. When he heard the news, Fletcher sank down on to the living-room sofa, momentarily speechless with shock and surprise.

'Of course . . . it's just possible that there may be sufficient detail in Brack's publication that was not included in the American article, isn't it?' he said weakly.

Seymour, tired and angry, shook his head and stared at Fletcher with open contempt.

'Doesn't sound like it,' he growled. 'And in any case wish-fulfilment is not part of my stock-in trade. We may not be high-powered academics, but we do try not to make stupid mistakes.'

'There was no indication in the files –'

'An irrelevant comment if ever I heard one. The fact is,' Seymour said brutally, 'that if the defence gets to know about Clarke's American article, then they can claim that the "secret" information which Brack is alleged to have revealed is in fact freely available to the general public on the other side of the Atlantic and has been so for six years. What I want to know, and now, is just how competent do you feel to answer such a case? You're supposed to be the expert, Dr Fletcher.'

Taken aback by the Special Branch man's sudden transformation from urbane helper to interrogator, Fletcher stared blankly at his shoes, unable to respond.

'Ah . . .' he said at last. 'I mean, is there actually any reason why the defence should get to know about Clarke's article?'

Before Seymour could begin to answer, they both heard the turning of a key in the front-door lock. The inspector held off, smiling inscrutably. Then Sarah Challen walked into the living room. She too was smiling, but her expression changed to one of wary surprise when she caught sight of Seymour.

'Oh, hello, darling,' Fletcher said, rising to his feet. His manner was carefully solicitous and guilty as hell. He was clearly glad to be let off the hook for the time being. 'Long time no see . . .' he stammered. 'Do you know Inspector Seymour?'

'No,' Sarah said. 'But I'd guessed.'

Seymour stood up and insisted on shaking hands with her, ignoring the chilly stare with which she greeted the gesture.

'You look as tired as I feel, Miss Challen,' he commented.

In the ensuing pause, Fletcher sat down again. It was a tactical mistake. Both Sarah and the inspector remained standing, weighing each other up in silence.

'Darling, the inspector has some disturbing information about . . .' Fletcher began awkwardly.

Seymour's interruption had a measure of calculated savagery, and he included Sarah in his audience as if she had been a participant all along.

'We have established that there was a period of association between Paul Brack and Simon Clarke while they were both in the United States some years ago,' he said. 'They shared many ideas, it would appear. And even if Brack has temporarily forgotten the relationship, the prospect of twenty years in prison might well concentrate his mind sufficiently to recall it – or at least the vital aspects – don't you think?'

Fletcher avoided his eyes and stared back at the carpet. Seymour's gaze switched to Sarah, who also looked away.

The inspector sighed patiently. 'In fact, there are already two people – so far as we know – who have taken the trouble to discover that Clarke is back in this country, and who have gone so far as to pay him a visit in the remote area where he now lives. One of them is my colleague Sergeant

Callaway, and the other, who managed to get there before him, is –' he took his time, watching them both keenly '– Sarah Challen.'

Fletcher seemed to sink deep into the upholstery of the sofa, waiting for it to swallow him up. He glared at Sarah with a mixture of pain, embarrassment and anger. Still she refused to confirm or deny anything.

'As I see it, you could have two reasons,' Seymour said to her, apparently unconcerned. It was one of the tricks of a policeman's trade to seem as though he had all the time in the world. 'Either,' he explained, 'you drove more than two hundred miles to try to buy Clarke's silence, in order to shore up the case against Brack; or you are trying to enlist Clarke's aid to secure Brack's release. Which is it, Miss Challen?' he asked comfortably, mild but somehow implacable.

Sarah walked over to the drinks table in the corner and poured herself a stiff gin. No more self-denial from now on; she needed this. Glass in hand, she faced Seymour and Fletcher once more and nodded slowly.

Seymour watched her with reluctant admiration, psychological interest overcoming his disgust at the mess this case was turning into. Miss Challen, he decided, was not only a rather beautiful young woman. She also had guts, and she was more than bright enough to realize what he and Fletcher had been discussing before she arrived on the scene. By now the inspector had no doubts about her motives for driving up to Wales; he just wanted it in plain English, particularly in front of Fletcher.

'I'm surprised either of you needs to ask that question,' Sarah Challen said at last, with a spectacularly withering glance in Fletcher's direction. She took a swallow from her drink. 'After all, that's what we want, isn't it?'

15

The old house, in mediaeval times a water mill, nestled at the foot of the Berkshire Downs. From the gardens, where a score of rare varieties of roses grew, an observer could see over to the Vale of the White Horse and beyond, almost to the plains of Wiltshire. The place was like a vision of peace, and yet on this warm spring afternoon two men sat at a wrought-iron table under the trees in that garden, long-empty coffee cups between them, discussing the end of mankind.

'How close to midnight would you put the hands of humanity's clock, Max?' Paul Brack asked quietly.

Maxwell Challen's lined face was solemn. He ran one hand through his sparse grey hair and sighed. 'Very close,' he said. 'Very close indeed . . .' Then he smiled at Brack, faintly but as if trying to provide some comfort. 'But in your generation there seems to be less false hope – the eternal enemy, the ostrich instinct. You have more awareness of . . . the connections . . . and of what the consequences of the holocaust would be.'

'Yes, I suppose that's something,' Brack said. 'And the next generation – my children – have even fewer illusions.'

He thought, as he spoke, of Angela and Oliver – and particularly of his son. There was a lot of work to be done there, and he had wasted time in a search for narrower truths. Things were different for young people these days; they had never chased the chimaera of limitless opportunities – and, growing up with the narrowing choices of the 1980s, probably never would.

'My great fear,' Brack continued after a pause. 'Is that they are also without belief in their ability to stop the inevitable.'

Challen looked out across the mill stream, nodding slowly, finding no words to counter Brack's statement. Like the younger man, he found the concept unthinkable.

It was Brack who broke the silence between them. 'So . . . where do I go from here, Max?' he murmured.

Challen frowned gently. 'It was presumptuous of me to advise you the first time, when you were still agonizing over whether to leave the AEA. I certainly would not presume to do so again – especially after this,' he added, tapping the copy of *The Brack Report* that had just been presented to him. 'No, you must plough your own furrow. But I will make one observation,' he said. The shrewdness of the veteran campaigner's glance was born of harsh experience. 'In the business of attempting to bring about change, the suffering you have to endure is directly proportional to the effectiveness of your action. Challen's Law. You are suffering prosecution now – and that is a clear indication that your Report has been effective.' He paused meaningfully. 'There is, however,' Challen continued, 'a limit to the amount of suffering you can take. You – and more especially your family.'

Brack waited for the next question. Evelyn Challen had left Max and married Norman Phillips. He had hardly known his own daughter until she was in her teens. The pain of Evelyn – and Sarah – went very deep, and could still surface in the old man at times like these. The question came.

'And how has Pat taken it all, Paul?' Challen asked.

'Bravely. And without much encouragement from me,' Brack conceded. He was astonished at the effort the admission cost him – which was precisely why the wily Challen had asked, he guessed. Sarah must have told her father quite a lot, or perhaps it was obvious to everyone except himself that he had been behaving like a bastard. Sarah and Pat. More unfinished business, fences to mend, futures to bring into being. So much to talk about, so little time. Brack looked at his watch. In fact, no time at all.

'I'm afraid I must go,' he said reluctantly. 'For my daily date with the police.'

'Of course.'

They walked slowly round the house to the gate, where Brack had left his bicycle after the ride from the station. The light was fading into evening, and there was a slight chill in the air now. Challen shivered involuntarily.

'I'm glad you didn't go to the States after Andrei Tchenkov, though I know that's what the authority were hankering after. I saw Tchenkov in Princeton last month. Unlike Edward Teller and Hans Bethe, he has not found his spiritual home. I doubt he will continue his work at the same level of brilliance, sad to say.'

The old man was waiting for Brack to finish putting on his bicycle clips.

'The Tchenkov business was a sad experience for Sarah, too. Have you . . . spoken to her since she came back?'

'No,' Brack said quickly, then felt ashamed of evading the issue. 'Well, she rang after the *Report* was published. It was nice to get a few words of encouragement from an old friend. That can be a commodity which suddenly becomes in short supply, as I'm sure you're well aware.'

'Ah . . .' was all Challen said to that, as if Brack had answered his question more fully than he needed to, which in a sense he had.

Challen held the five-bar gate open while Brack wheeled his bike out into the road. Holding the bike steady with one hand, Brack waved cheerfully in the direction of a parked car fifty yards or so away. The man reading a newspaper in the front seat glanced up briefly, then looked away.

'My escort,' Brack explained. He paused shyly. 'When I first came down to Farden Mill all that time ago, you said to me: "Every decision is an act of repression. We pursue one course of action only by repressing myriad alternatives."' He smiled. 'Watch me try to beat the house rules, Max. . . .'

Challen chuckled and patted him on the shoulder. 'If there's anything I can do to help with the defence. . . . But then with my reputation, I'm afraid I'd be more of a liability to you.'

'I'm not much of an asset myself. Why worry?' Brack answered, climbing onto his bike.

'Well, give my regards to Harold. And when it's over, if you're able, come down and relax for a few days. Bring the family. . . .'

Brack's farewell smile broadened. Challen understood that bit, too. 'Thank you, Max. And good-bye,' he said, leaning over to shake the old man's hand.

'Good-bye, Paul. And good luck.'

Challen watched while Brack cycled off down the road towards the station in the twilight. The parked car turned sedately in Brack's wake, and followed him.

He stayed standing there until the younger man was out of sight, then walked slowly back to the garden table, inspecting one or two of the newer rose bushes on the way. The copy of *The Brack Report* was still lying there, shiny, its pages crisp and unread. Challen weighed it up in his hand, sat down and opened it.

The first page was inscribed, in Paul Brack's handwriting: 'To Max Challen, with love and in hope.'

Despite the cool of the evening, Max Challen sat gazing at the inscription for some time, and the corners of his lined eyes were moist with emotion.

Pat Brack arrived on her daily visit early the next morning. She had been strong, and when the children had come over for lunch she and Brack had contrived to keep the atmosphere light and jokey. This time was different, though. As soon as he opened the door, her husband could see the strain was really starting to tell on her. Pat slumped in a chair, accepted a cup of coffee with a wordless nod. When Brack sat down, too, he saw tears gathering.

'What's the problem, love?' he murmured.

Pat laughed, a harsh sound mirroring the near-hysteria

that was flowing over her. 'Paul, I'm not sure I can carry on taking it – the constant questions. . . .'

'They can't do you any harm, love.'

'But when am I going to be rid of him, Paul?' she said haltingly. 'I have an almost daily dose. Questions about trivial domestic things, events that happened ten, fifteen years ago that I can hardly remember straight any more. I've even been asked about your political affiliations at Cambridge – and they won't believe you didn't have any.'

Brack smiled. 'Ah well, that's part of the cross we have to bear, you know.'

'It's not actually that funny from the receiving end!' Pat snapped.

Brack swirled his half-drunk coffee round in its mug, and said quietly: 'I think it's *me* who's on the receiving end, isn't it?'

'Technically, certainly,' Pat interrupted, anger flaring up to replace despair. 'I know you have a totally solipsistic, self-centred view of the world, but I am, as they say, suspect by association. If you thrive on persecution, I most certainly don't – and I could do with just an occasional touch of appreciation for what I have to suffer on your behalf. . . .'

He moved towards her. 'Oh, Pat . . .' Challen had been right. He knew what he was doing, but someone in his wife's position could take only just so much without cracking.

They sat holding each other while Pat's anger ebbed.

'If we have to go through this, Paul, please let's go through it together,' she stammered. 'I . . . I just can't handle it on my own. They sit there . . . in my house, where we have . . . after all . . . had some happy times together, and . . . I don't know . . . they make me feel dirty.'

He nodded, stroking her hair.

'I can't help it, when you're so far away,' Pat continued in a small, bleak voice. 'They make the most vile insinuations. It's as though they're talking about someone else, some monster you might read about in the paper. . . . And then I look up and see Callaway's cold little eyes boring into me, and I realize . . . well, that he's talking about you, my husband . . .'

Brack got up suddenly and took a couple of steps away from her. He needed to distance himself, whatever the cost. Otherwise he would never get the chance to think this through.

'What kind of things does he say about me, love?' he asked, gently but firmly.

Pat shrugged. 'Oh, the same ghosts I've lived with for years. That you're a charlatan, a glory-seeker, not really a proper scientist at all. You know the kind of thing.'

'You've faced it all before, Pat,' he said, nodding sour agreement.

'Yes,' she answered. 'But not from a grubby little policeman with a mind like a sewer.'

Try to get a sense of proportion into things, Brack thought. Keep it light, because once you gave in to them you were lost. 'I've always found the good Inspector Seymour rather sympathetic,' he said, and made a face. The sally fell flat.

'Well,' Pat retorted sullenly. 'I've had Callaway, and I can assure you he's no joke.' She sighed. 'And when the context is a charge of treason, the insinuations are very powerful – in an insidious sort of way.'

Brack looked at her in pained astonishment. 'You're more inclined to believe them?'

'No. Nor have I ever done. That was never the issue,' Pat said quickly. She got to her feet and stood facing him. 'But I'm human, Paul – perhaps too much so for your taste. From time to time I need a little reassurance. And in the face of attacks by men like Callaway, I need more. A lot more.'

But Brack wasn't quite ready to take the step back towards her yet.

'What else have the prosecutors found to throw at me?' he asked sardonically. 'That I'm sexually promiscuous?'

There was pain in his wife's eyes, though her words were

matter-of-fact. 'Oh yes,' she said. 'I've had all of that.'

A brief pause, then Brack nodded. 'You're right. We should be sharing all this, not shadow-boxing at long distance.' He smiled. 'What do I do about getting a change of venue to report? How long will it take to get the whole stupid business transferred to Oxford?'

'You mean . . . you'll come home?'

'If we can arrange it with the police.'

Pat stepped over and kissed him impulsively on the cheek. 'Paul, thank you,' she said.

Their embrace was unhurried, and without self-consciousness for the first time in months, perhaps even years.

'I'll make some more coffee,' Brack laughed. 'A chaste celebration of the homecoming – or homegoing. . . .'

He called out from the kitchen: 'I saw Max Challen yesterday.'

Pat grinned. 'He must be impressed with his protégé's performance. Probably green with envy!'

They were both still laughing together when there was an insistent knock at the door. Brack told Pat to wait and came out of the kitchen to answer.

'Might be bovver-boy Callaway,' he said darkly. 'Forgot to ask you where I buy my underpants.'

Pat struggled to keep smiling, but she could feel the tension returning. Her husband opened the door, and there was something about the way he stiffened. . . .

In the event, the voice she heard was Sarah Challen's. Sarah obviously didn't realize she was here, and Brack said nothing at first.

'Hello, Paul,' she heard Sarah say. 'The door was open downstairs, so I came straight up. . . . You see, I've found something that could help you.'

Pat stepped forward so that she could see Sarah and the other woman could see her. Brack stood uncertainly between them, and Sarah's face held the same mixture of guilt and suppressed resentment that she had seen the last time, outside the inquiry hall.

'Don't worry. I . . . I'll leave,' Pat said.

Brack shook his head emphatically. 'No, don't Pat, please.' But he made no move towards her and away from Sarah.

'I see,' Pat said. She hated the poison she could feel in her own voice, even as she spoke. This was too much, though – it had to come out. 'Jealousy may be out of fashion in the single girls' magazines, but I still find it hard to cope with,' she hissed. She walked out between them and on to the landing, without looking back.

Brack made to follow her down the stairs. Sarah put an urgent hand on his arm.

'Pat won't listen at the moment, Paul,' she said softly. 'I know how she feels. There'll be time enough for explanations later.'

He hesitated, then smiled. 'Yes,' he said. 'Time. That's a valuable thing. Can you promise to give me some?'

Sarah did not answer immediately. She went past him and into the room. 'Not me,' she said. 'Someone else entirely, someone who seems to have slipped the infallible Brack memory. . . .'

Brack closed the door with some reluctance and followed her into the room. Choices again, he thought. Always choices, for God's sake.

'Okay,' Harlan said. 'You've picked up some smut on the man who did the original summary on laser enrichment for the AEA all that time ago?'

John Foster nodded and looked at his notes. 'A few pointers.'

Harlan glanced at Alan Stevenson. The solicitor's comments so far had not been too optimistic, so what Foster had to say could be crucial.

'A brief outline, then,' he told the inquiry agent. 'Alan's got plenty to do, and so have I. It's after eleven, and I still haven't had time to sort through my mail, let alone make any phone calls.'

Foster took the point. His master's voice. 'Well,' he began. 'This chap Clarke went to the States to work for the

Westinghouse Corporation – and he was there during the later part of Brack's own sojourn there. That we knew already. What I have managed to find out, however, is that Clarke got involved with some maverick academic types. I've heard them variously described as anarchists, revolutionaries, liberals – it all depends on your prejudice, I daresay,' he explained primly. 'Anyway, they called themselves the Alternative Scientists, and they published a radical science journal from their base in New England with the title of *Custard* Pi.'

Foster grinned, found no takers for humour, and continued hastily:

'Pi as in pi-r-squared, of course. Now, Clarke has sunk without trace, but there's just a chance he may have contributed to the magazine. It specialized in cocking a snook at the establishment, and since laser enrichment was very much his field, he's very likely to have written about it. . . .'

Harlan frowned and looked sceptical, though he was clearly interested. 'I would have thought that if he'd published information which was that secret there would have been quite a scandal. Someone would have picked him up, surely?'

'Not necessarily,' Foster answered. 'American information and secrecy laws are rather looser than ours, as you probably know. And I've also discovered that the average world-wide readership for a learned article in a specialist journal is – wait for it – three.' He chuckled dryly, proud of his research. 'That's a result of a survey by the Information Institute, just published this year.'

'He's right,' Stevenson agreed. 'I've read something similar myself. The essential requirement for making a career is publication – which has nothing to do with anyone actually reading what you write. But then surely Paul himself would know about the material if it had got into print? He was one of the small, specialized circle.'

'He knew about the original, classified material itself from his old days at the AEA, of course,' Foster countered.

'In any case, he left the States not so long after Clarke got involved with the Alternative Scientist crowd. It's possible that anything Clarke wrote was not published until after Brack returned to the UK.'

Stevenson nodded. 'Well, it's an interesting line – and we could do with a new element in the case.' He sighed. 'When can you check it out fully?'

Foster smiled at Harlan. 'The quickest way would be for me to go over and do the looking on the spot.'

Harlan's answering grunt was non-committal. 'Okay, so you want an expenses-paid trip to America,' he growled. 'But the prospect is still theoretical, and we don't even have any assurance that the man Clarke actually wrote anything. You say he's disappeared?'

'At first sight, it seems so.'

'Blackballed, perhaps. They may have nothing so crude as the Official Secrets Act in the Land of the Free, but they know how to give a man a hard time if he steps out of line. I know that from my own time in the oil business . . .'

'I'm pretty sure I could find him,' Foster persisted.

Harlan, however, continued to stall. 'All right,' he said. 'But are there any other possibilities of this kind? I mean, why not have another go at Paul and see if you can jog his memory? Perhaps you could be there, too, Alan . . .?'

There was a discreet knock at the door.

'Enter!' Harlan shouted.

Sophie Ferris slipped into the room, half-closing the door behind her. She seemed flustered.

'Excuse me for butting in,' Sophie said. 'But I have Paul here, together with Sarah Challen, of all people. He seems very impatient to have a word with you about something.'

The three men looked at each other with irrational embarrassment, like well-meaning gossips caught red-handed.

Before Sophie had a chance to block his way, Paul Brack had sidled through the gap behind her and into the office.

'Come on, Harold,' he chided gaily. 'I think we can interrupt the ninety-third high-level briefing of the week under these circumstances. This is important – to everyone.'

'Now wait a minute,' Harlan objected. 'I thought I said we'd do this my way . . .'

Ignoring him, Brack turned and beckoned to Sarah Challen to join him.

'Hello, Harold,' she said sweetly.

'Good morning, Sarah.' Harlan's greeting had all the welcoming quality of a blast of grape-shot.

Meanwhile, Brack had wrested Sarah's briefcase from her grip and was hastily opening it.

'I see your command of the social graces has not deserted you, Harold,' he said wryly.

Brack walked over to Harlan's desk and dropped something onto it. The object was a slim, cyclostyled bulletin, A4-sized and printed on poor-quality paper, with a crude cartoon of an exploding product of the baker's craft alongside what passed for a mast-head.

'Here we are,' he announced. 'Courtesy of Ms Sarah Challen, her father's daughter, a very tasty little number called *Custard* Pi.'

16

Norman Phillips parked his car in the space reserved for official visitors, locked it and proceeded into the building. He noticed in passing that Braintree's ministerial Princess was parked on its usual space. Good, he thought grimly: no delays. He had something to deliver and a little to say, and both items he wanted over quickly. Pretty soon he intended to take a holiday, get a chance to do some unencumbered thinking.

Phillips had his briefcase checked at the reception desk by the security man, then stepped into the lift and pressed the button for the top floor.

He was ushered straight into Braintree's office, where the Secretary of State was sitting at his desk, deep in some papers.

'Ah . . . Norman,' Braintree said, glancing up to acknowledge his arrival. Ministerial smiles of welcome, like most government property, came in several grades. This one was of pretty mediocre quality, a presagement of what was to come. Braintree came straight to what, as far as he could judge, was the point of the meeting. 'So we've got no case against Brack after all?' he opened.

'So I hear,' Phillips answered icily.

'Do sit down . . .'

Phillips shook his head. 'For the moment I feel happier on my feet, Minister. You see, I've not come to talk about Brack. I think his importance has lessened somewhat.'

In answer to Braintree's enquiring look, he fished into

his briefcase and pulled out a thick typescript, which he carefully put down on the minister's desk.

Braintree peered at it suspiciously.

'This looks very . . . weighty and serious, Norman,' he said. 'What might it be?'

'A report,' Phillips said simply, dropping Braintree's courtesy title. 'The report of the committee we set up to investigate the implications of the earthquake at Wintersham two years ago.'

'And it's not good, I suppose,' Braintree said. 'Give me the . . . er . . . bottom line.'

Phillips shrugged. 'The damaged "A" reactor is beyond economic repair. It cannot be safely sealed without damaging the "B" reactor twinned with it.' He took a deep breath, looking Braintree straight in the eye. 'To cut a long story short, the committee's recommendation is that the entire power station should be dismantled and that the reactor cores should be concrete-sealed for perpetuity.'

Then he sat down abruptly.

'Oh God,' Braintree said, the colour draining from his well-bred face. Ignoring the fact that Phillips had just taken the proffered seat, he got up and looked out of the window, shifting from foot to foot in his agitation. 'You realize the implications of this?'

'I imagine,' Phillips said slowly, 'that you're going to tell me it's the final nail in the coffin of the AGR programme?'

Braintree snorted in despair and swung round to face him, suddenly accusing.

'How long has this been brewing?' he snarled. The smooth façade had cracked, to reveal the bare-knuckle political prizefighter beneath the surface.

'We had the report this morning,' Phillips answered calmly, refusing to be intimidated.

'But you must have had some idea what to expect?'

'As you know, there has been speculation ever since the earthquake and the consequent trouble at the power station. We have been liaising with senior men in your department, including Sir Frank Sampson, on developments. But, of course, until the report actually came in . . .'

Braintree interrupted angrily. 'Yes, yes . . . but that doesn't serve to excuse a fiasco of this magnitude. How on earth can we have got into the position of protecting the Heathbridge AGR Inquiry from a man like Brack, when . . .'

He stopped. Something in the Secretary of State's memory had clicked, and he stared at Phillips in horrified wonder.

'Wait a minute, Norman,' he said. 'Correct me if I'm wrong, but wasn't Brack directly involved at Wintersham?'

'He was, minister. I spoke to him personally the morning after the trouble with the core.'

Braintree groaned and smashed one fist against his palm in frustration.

'Dear God, and we can't even stop him from crowing!'

Phillips had noted with intense interest Braintree's reference to 'protecting' the Heathbridge Inquiry from Paul Brack. He hoped no one in authority ever found out what had really tracked down Simon Clarke and come up with the back number of that obscure American magazine. His step-daughter was going to have quite enough problems rearranging her professional and private life without that kind of unpleasantness.

For now, however, Phillips concentrated on the spectacle of the Rt. Hon. Basil Braintree blowing a fuse. It was neither a pleasant nor an edifying sight.

'Oh, I doubt if Brack will be doing much crowing, Minister,' he said in an attempt to mollify him. 'He knows too much about the way things are arranged, and he's no lover of the American PWRs which the Electricity Generating Board will inevitably demand now to fill the gaps in their reactor programme.'

Phillips concluded with a wintry smile. Braintree, still on his feet, eyed him sullenly.

'A whole heap more trouble, I suppose,' he growled.

'An inconvenient but – happily – inevitable consequence of living in a free society, don't you agree, Minister?' Phillips said.

Braintree chose not to answer. He leaned over and pressed a button on his desk intercom.

'Is Sir Frank in?' he asked. 'Good. Well, when he's finished I want him in here. Soonest.'

He clicked the machine off. 'Frank Sampson helped get me into this,' he said, as if to himself. 'Now he can draft a press statement that gets us all out again.'

Sarah Challen and Brian Fletcher had spent half an hour talking about principles, while other, personal questions hovered like hyenas waiting to move in on a corpse.

Fletcher, sitting distanced from her across the far side of the living room in Sarah's flat, was still raising a head of steam over Brack's 'betrayal'.

'Whichever way you look at it,' he said, 'it is totally irresponsible to spread around the idea that any competent high-school physicist can make a nuclear bomb.'

'Can you deny it's true?' Sarah retorted.

Fletcher tapped his foot in exasperation and said nothing.

'If it's possible,' she continued, 'then it will be done, and never mind whether it makes the front page of the *Daily Express*. And if you ask me – which you haven't, never have – the lack of responsibility should be laid at the door of those people in authority who have connived to litter the surface of this planet with materials capable of destroying it. That's why *I*, at least, was interested in fusion.'

'Oh, wake up to yourself, Sarah,' Fletcher muttered. 'Your main interest in the beauties of fusion was Paul Brack.'

There it was suddenly, the real question, Sarah thought. She had to be honest and get it over quickly.

'Yes,' she said slowly. 'That *was* true. . . .'

Fletcher snorted. 'It is still! And you're behaving like a

spoilt child, determined to get what you can't have, whatever the cost for everyone else.' He glanced at her, saw she was not bothering to deny it, and subsided again. 'Morally, Brack was in the wrong on this issue, and you let him off the hook,' he said.

Sarah found herself looking at him with complete dispassion. Perhaps that was the real end of love, she mused. Seeing another human for the first time as he or she really was, and then not being able to take it. Brian's handsome face hadn't changed, and she had always tolerated his lack of subtle understanding, but both seemed ugly to her now. He too was a spoilt child – not a privileged one like her, but ruined, always wanting, just the same.

'I shouldn't have got into this relationship, Brian,' she said quietly. 'I did it for all the wrong reasons. Yes, I am spoilt, in some ways a child. But I have to learn to live alone and heal the hurt through my own resources, not cover it with a band-aid second best. . . .'

'Gosh, thanks,' Fletcher answered with bitter sarcasm. 'That's good to know.'

Why did it have to end like this? Sarah felt like simply walking out and telling Fletcher to be out by the time she got back. In some respects that would be kinder. Nevertheless, she pressed on, knowing she owed some kind of explanation, both to him and to herself.

'No, Paul Brack wasn't important in the way you think,' she said. 'More significant was the fact that you wanted to suppress him. You thought you could challenge him intellectually, and when you realized his superior strength you reached for a clumsy weapon to hold him down and stop his mouth. Certainly I have wanted Paul – and I still do, if I'm honest with myself. But in tracking down Simon Clarke I was attempting to release a fellow-scientist whom I respect from the grip of a law which I despise.'

Sarah paused before delivering the final blow. Fletcher was staring vacantly into his drink, waiting. She knew she had to say it, and deep down she knew she wanted it to hit hard, even hurt.

'You see,' she told him. 'I see now that I despise anyone who could seek to use that law to suppress a threatening truth. That's why we can't go on.'

17

The steps leading up to the main entrance of Waldegrave House were crowded with journalists and camera men. The ones who could not get close enough to Paul Brack were busy surveying and taking pictures of the weird and wonderful phenomena in the grounds. Windmills, strange plants, solar panels – good stuff to pad out the gaps in tomorrow's double-page spreads, 'NUKE REBEL RETURNS TO HIS MANSION OF THE FUTURE', that sort of thing.

At that moment Brack stood a few yards from the main door, talking into a microphone held by Nick Rowe of ITN. Harlan and Alan Stevenson hovered just out of camera shot, listening keenly as he gave his reaction to this morning's announcement about the AGR programme.

'Of course, I'm delighted that the country, and Heathbridge in particular, has had this burden lifted from it,' he said. 'I think we can be grateful that the Wintersham Inquiry has shaken off its initial complacency – which I can regrettably vouch for, since I was there at the time. More comment when I hear the details, but it's certainly good news, as far as it goes.'

Rowe nodded. 'As far as it goes. . . . So how do you see the future of nuclear power in this country, Dr Brack?'

'The battleground will now shift to the inquiry which is promised for later this year into the CEGB's proposal to build Britain's first American Pressurized Water Reactor,' Brack answered. 'The government's statement, as usual, is a masterpiece of fudging the issues, but I think the way ahead is clear enough – at least for the PWR's opponents. We have made the case against, we must ensure that it is forcefully advocated, and we trust that the proposal will be decisively rejected on the basis of free and open discussion of the evidence. Only then will we be able to say that we have taken our first, tentative step as a nation towards securing a lasting future for this Planet Earth of ours. . . .'

Harlan was making signals, but Rowe slipped in another question quickly:

'Mr George Spiking, leader of TUCANE, has already entered the lists for the PWR Inquiry, fresh from Heathbridge. He professes great admiration for you. What part do you see yourself, personally, playing in the coming campaign?'

Brack smiled and opened his mouth to speak, but at that moment Harlan bawled: 'Cut!'

The camera crew did just that, automatically responding to the order. Rowe peered round in dismay as Harlan moved in and took Brack by the arm.

'No more, Paul,' Harlan said firmly. He turned to the ITN team. 'That's it. End of story,' he declared. 'Thanks, fellows. Look forward to seeing it on the box.'

He began to steer Brack towards the door. Rowe shook his head. 'Keeping a tight rein on him, are you, Mr Harlan?' he called out when they reached the entrance.

Harlan turned and grinned, returning the reporter's cynicism with interest, and with that Paul Brack, flanked by his boss and Alan Stevenson, walked into Waldegrave House and out of the public eye.

There were perhaps a couple of dozen people, all carefully checked by hired security staff, gathered in Harlan's office when he uncorked the champagne. Brack's colleagues at Harlan International made up the bulk, along with Stevenson, John Foster, Sophie Ferris – and Sarah Challen.

Harlan beamed as he held the foaming bottle aloft. 'Enjoy!' he urged them. 'Because after this there'll be plenty of work for you idle lot to get on with!'

The glasses were handed round amid laughter and applause. Harlan stepped out of the centre of attention, his host's work done, and headed for Alan Stevenson.

'Thanks a lot, Alan,' he said, shaking him by the hand. 'Good work. We made it – in spite of the client's full determination to commit public hara-kiri.'

Stevenson nodded and sipped his champagne. 'Yes, it was a darned close-run thing.' He looked ruefully at Harlan. 'How are you going to control him from now on, Harold? We can't always be nursemaiding him around.'

Harlan waved a hand expansively. 'How do you control the sea, or a volcano? The most you can do is try and siphon off some of the by-products,' he said. He was grinning as he spoke, but the slight edge of unease was still there. 'I don't know, Alan,' he admitted. 'In fact, I haven't the faintest idea yet what precisely I am going to do with him. Hey . . . where is he?'

Harlan looked across the room and called to Sophie Ferris, who was over by the door:

'You haven't lost him already, have you, Sophie?'

His PA pointed in the direction of her own office and winked. 'He's on the phone. To home, I think. . . .'

At her side, Sarah Challen was chatting with John Foster. She continued to do so with every appearance of relaxed sociability, but a keen observer would have noticed the fleeting look of strained concern that crossed her face when she heard Sophie's cheerful words.

Brack, in fact, was sitting with his feet up on Sophie Ferris's desk, waiting for an answer from the Oxford number he had dialled. It took some twenty seconds to come, a tired-sounding 'hello'.

He launched straight in without bothering to introduce himself. 'Pat. What are you doing skulking at home on such a fine spring afternoon as this?'

'Paul!' the voice said, no longer quite so weary.

Brack smiled to himself, pressing the mouthpiece closer to shut out the din from the party next door.

'The charge has been dropped, love,' he told her. 'And

the Heathbridge Inquiry is adjourned pending an urgent government policy review. How about that?'

'No! I can't believe it!' Pat squealed, making him wince and move the phone away from his ear again. 'How has all this happened?' she continued, a little more subdued. 'I suppose you have Sarah to thank for your good fortune.'

'*Our* good fortune,' he corrected her. 'For some of it, yes. But Pat . . .'

'Sorry about this morning, if that's what you were going to mention. I over-reacted.'

Brack raised his eyes to the ceiling in relief. 'I'm glad you did. Sorry you had to. If you understand what I mean. . . .'

The silence on both ends of the line that followed somehow managed to say more than a hundred wordy protestations of undying love and reconciliation.

'So, what now?' Pat said after a few moments, tenderly but with an undertone of urgency.

'Oh, I'm not even thinking of that,' Brack answered. 'Not until I've discussed it with you.'

Pat chuckled. 'Liar!'

'Not at all,' he protested. 'And the first confirmation I want from you is: are you expecting me for supper?'

Sarah Challen was standing alone, staring through the elegant window at the grounds, when Harlan crept up on her.

'Hello, Sarah,' he said, smiling in a most unchivalrous fashion at her start of surprise. 'How does it feel to be mingling with the dissident minority? Last time, when Paul was thinking of leaving the AEA to work for me, it was me and Max against you.'

She examined him coolly. 'What do you really think, Harold. Were there winners and losers?'

'Depends,' Harlan said, 'on what you consider a winning score.'

Sarah gestured with her champagne glass in the direction of the door of Sophie's office.

'Well, he's his own man at last, Harold,' she murmured. 'No one owns him now. I'd guess that must have been hard for you, of all people, to accept.'

'Harder for you, I think,' Harlan answered, making it clear that he had known all along about her feelings for Brack and wasn't in the business of making judgements. 'At least Harlan International has *The Brack Report.*'

'We all have that. And was it a sound investment?'

Harlan considered briefly, then gave her an answer she could hardly have expected. 'He's a difficult man to know,' he said. 'But you don't have a monopoly of that privilege.'

He was looking past her as he spoke, smiling in a way that seemed to encourage and warn at the same time. Sarah turned, followed his gaze and saw Brack approaching through the throng, relaxed and waving in their direction. Harlan moved forward to meet him.

'Paul, let me get you a glass of something madly intoxicating,' he said. 'Do yourself a favour. Cloud that over-active brain of yours just a little.'

Brack laughed dutifully. 'Thank you, Harold. That might not be a bad idea.'

Harlan made his way over to the drinks bar, where he slipped effortlessly into conversation with Veejay Patel.

Brack watched him with dour affection, then turned back to Sarah. 'And thank you, Sarah,' he said.

They embraced fleetingly and chastely.

'I suppose everybody's asking you what you intend to do next, Paul,' Sarah said then, and it was a statement rather than a question.

Brack inclined his head and smiled.

'And I hear you went to see Max?' she continued.

'Yes, I did.'

Sarah looked down at her glass. 'That was very sweet of you.'

'What a dreadful way of putting it,' Brack answered. 'No, I went because I had to. Max is a very important influence in my life . . . one of very few,' he admitted.

She acknowledged the rare morsel of self-criticism, then looked at him with a sudden intensity. 'Just don't make the same mistake, though, Paul.'

They stood and looked at each other, reliving their past, in a sense: their work together; their affair; her warnings to him about leaving the AEA and going into the wilderness, the bitterness over the treatment of Andrei Tchenkov.

'Oh, history never repeats itself . . . quite,' Brack said. 'There's too many people changing it all the time . . . when it isn't busy changing us.' He switched subjects quickly. 'Speaking of which, what about you, Sarah?'

The question was more than mere social chit-chat, but something in his expression told her that it had no emotional overtones. Sarah took the hint.

'I'm on my own,' she replied, hoping the regret was not too obvious. 'Personally certainly, perhaps even professionally, though there's still a decision to be made in that department. Learning to live with that will take a little while. But at the moment it's what I need to do.'

'Yes,' Brack agreed gently. 'It's an essential first base – which too many of the needers resent. You have to get through that one before things really become possible, before you're fully capable of making your own choices. . . .'

Harlan had obviously decided that they had been given enough time to say what had to be said. He was back, with a full bottle and a glass for Brack.

'Here you are,' he announced, pouring a generous measure into Brack's glass and then topping up his own and Sarah's.

They drank.

'Well . . .?' Harlan said.

Brack raised a quizzical eyebrow. 'Do I take it, Harold, that you're asking me to come up with something of significance?'

Harlan smiled his predator's smile. '*The Brack Report* will do.'

Each, perhaps for different reasons, drank a toast to that one.

Brack wheeled his bicycle away from the barrier and out into the forecourt of Oxford station. The night was cool, with a slight breeze in the air. He climbed slowly on to the bike, still feeling the effects of the afternoon's champagne, and set off through the dark streets to cover the two miles or so to the house.

He cycled at an easy pace, leaving himself some time to think. It felt good and right to be travelling here on the most harmless, cheapest, most efficient means of transport known to man, for the ancient university city was still a cyclist's town, home of the young, bright, and temporarily poor. He had often wondered, and he wondered again now as he met undergraduates on their well-used machines, what a difference it would make if the whole of the western world agreed to be even a little bit poorer for three, four years – not to work for some degree that they would probably never even use, but to save the earth's resources. Hopelessly idealistic, of course, even to consider the thought: tell people to give up their luxuries for a positive goal and they laughed you to scorn or called you a revolutionary; ask them to undergo all manner of privations in order to win a war, a pointless contest of mutual destruction, and they would do it willingly.

His route took him round the corner of Gloucester Green, past Worcester College, and along the whole length of Walton Street to the point where it became Kingston Road and the northern suburbs, terraced houses skirting the grand Victorian residences, began. At the Rose and Crown, not so far from home, he was tempted to stop off and look in, lured by the thought of a good glass of beer and the chance of seeing and listening to students again. He had to press on, of course, but comforted himself with the fact that he could take Angela and Oliver out for a drink any night soon. Oliver was old enough to go in pubs now. They would be able to talk without feeling trapped and threatened by each other. And perhaps the same went for Pat.

Twenty minutes after leaving the station, Brack pedalled up the drive to the house, refreshed by the ride, his mind feeling clearer than it had for days. He propped the bike up by the back door, locked it out of habit – though there was no real need here – and let himself quietly into the house with his key. For several moments he stood still in the back hall, enjoying anticipation of the surprise he was about to give his family, testing the feel of the place after his absence. Good. It no longer felt like a trap. Here he would still have choices, he thought. Here one could expect – and give – support.

Pat, Angela and Oliver were in the living room watching television. No one looked up when he gently opened the connecting door. Brack soon gauged the reason: his own image, his public face, was dominating the TV screen.

'Only then,' his other self was saying, 'will we be able to say that we have taken our first, tentative step towards a lasting future for this Planet Earth. . . .'

He could see that his family approved, and he was glad. It gave him a dryer, double-edged pleasure to see them frown as Nick Rowe, the interviewer, explained:

'My interview with Dr Brack was cut short by Harold Harlan, his employer. But it's difficult to believe that we have heard the last word from this controversial scientist.'

Angela, turning to pick up a coffee cup from the table by her armchair, was the first to notice his presence.

'Dad!' she shouted.

Oliver glanced over and smiled a greeting as casually as if his father had simply been out for the day.

Pat walked slowly over and turned off the television set before she faced him.

Brack stood there in his cycle clips, hair still wild from his ride through Oxford. 'I've still no idea what to do next,' he said. 'But I've come home to think about it.'

His wife's smile was ironic, with no room for illusions.

'You're welcome, you horrible man,' she said. 'Though sometimes I think you're easier to live with on television.'

Then she ran forward to put her arms around Brack, just to make sure that he didn't take her words too seriously.